Demise of a Devious Suspect

A River's Edge Cozy Mystery

Third in the Series

Elaine L. Orr

©2018 Annie Acorn Publishing LLC
Silver Spring, MD 20906
annieacornpublishing.com

ISBN: 9781730964343

Cover Art by Angel Nichols
nicholsangel86@yahoo.com
http://www.angelwingsdesigner.com/bookcovers.htm

Disclaimer

Demise of a Devious Suspect by Elaine Orr is a work of fiction. Any character resemblance to real people or events is completely accidental. A few literary liberties may have been taken when it comes to some geographic locations in the interest of creating great literature.

Acknowledgments

As always, I appreciate the Decatur Critique Group and their spot-on comments on characters and plot. Thanks to Karen Musser Nortman, a super beta reader. Special thanks to Bill Reese of Reese's Funeral Home in Ottumwa, Iowa for advice on cremation.

CHAPTER ONE

THE MOST PEACEFUL ASPECT of that Friday evening on the front porch was the certainty that my problems were over. My brother Ambrose and I had secured full rights to our late parents' property, and I had a free place to live. He could farm without renting land. We were home.

I was, anyway. Ambrose and his wife Sharon planned to continue living close to Dubuque, where she taught school. Except for spring planting and fall harvest, my brother would work the land by coming to Southeast Iowa a few days each month. I could manage the farm other times.

The front porch of my late parents' house, now ours, faced the wide yard that separated it from a tall barn and its surrounding cornfield. The dried stalks would soon come face to face with a combine, and my view across our fields would be unobstructed.

Coming back to River's Edge after college in Iowa City hadn't been my first plan, but jobs in journalism aren't plentiful if you want to stay in Iowa. I was happy at the *South County News*. At least, until Hal Morris fired me.

I smiled. Who would have thought I'd be glad that happened? I loved the landscaping business I started last year. I worked hard, but my time was my own. Now that we had the farm again, I needed a flexible schedule.

A bark near my feet announced that Mister Tibbs had awakened from her after-dinner nap.

I leaned over to pet her wiry curls. "Hello, girl. You want to walk to the barn and back?" I still didn't let her roam without me. Probably would after she learned how to find her way home from a cornfield. Once you're in one, every stalk looks alike, and with her being mostly a terrier mix, I'd never spot her.

Mister Tibbs, so named because her prior owner wanted a boy and kept the name she had planned for one, trotted ahead of me to the barn. Her routine has become to walk around and then through it, usually making a deposit at the edge of the cornfield. My unscientific survey will determine whether the stalks in that area grow taller than those nearby.

As we rounded the barn to return to the house a smart-looking, dark green pickup pulled onto the lot. I can't say driveway, because the middle of the large yard is simply where we park.

Syl Seaton was my first client as a landscaper. I waved at him and walked to his truck. "What brings you to the hinterlands at dusk?"

He grinned. "Hello, Melanie. Finished a big segment of a project and wanted to get the heck out of my house."

He lives on several acres at the far western side of River's Edge. He's never said why he moved to Iowa from California. More specifically, why River's Edge. He got some kind of big IT contract with an insurance firm in Des Moines, but our town is nearly ninety miles from there.

Syl held up two bottles of my favorite beer. "Nightcap?"

"By all means." We turned and walked in quiet companionship to the side porch. Mister Tibbs, still on her long leash, led the way and plopped on the recently painted gray floorboards, panting lightly.

I gestured that Syl should sit in one of the two canvas chairs. "I should shop for some real furniture, but I'm in no rush."

He twisted the cap on one of the beers and passed it to me before he sat. "I expect you have more important things to think about."

"But nothing unpleasant. Since the fields were rented out for this season, I'm mostly working with Ambrose to buy some additional equipment for next year, get repairs made to the barn, that kind of thing."

Syl nodded at the brilliantly red maple tree that sat on the west side of the house. "Those leaves mean you won't have much to do 'til spring."

I laughed. "Spoken like a city guy. Lots of winter chores. Order seeds, map out what to plant next year. I'm going to paint most of the rooms in the house. I want it to look…different."

He nodded at a folder on the floor next to my chair. "Going to finish Hal's book?"

I snorted. "Not hardly."

Before his untimely death, Hal had been secretly writing a novel about a local farm couple who had been killed in a car accident. Aside from the few chapters being some of the most poorly written I'd read, he had extrapolated the circumstances of my parents' accident to imply they had been murdered by someone who wanted to buy their land. If Hal hadn't been dead when someone gave me his draft, I'd have killed him.

"Why do you have it out?"

I picked up the folder and pointed to my name, which was scrawled on the front. "You remember I told you this came to me because Bruce Blackner found it when he bought Hal's old boat?"

Syl nodded. "Yep."

"Hal had no family, so when Bruce saw my name, he figured Hal had been working with me on it."

Syl laughed. "Maybe that's a reason to finish it for your late and, as I understand it, largely unmourned, former boss?"

"No way. I showed it to Sandi a few weeks ago. She can't think of any reason Hal wrote my name on it, so we decided he was simply making a note to himself to call me." I nodded at the manuscript. "I'm trying to talk myself into trashing it."

"And why is that so hard?"

"I'm sure not sentimental about Hal, but it's hard to toss what might be the last project he worked on. I wish he had relatives I could give it to."

"You're journalists. Doesn't one of you know contests for tackiest first chapters?"

I grinned. "Probably, but I doubt this would even be up to snuff for that. I should invite Sandi over, and we can toss it into the burn barrel behind the house. Watch it go up in flames."

We sat in silence as we drank the beer. Syl's expression seemed more solemn than usual. Though he's not exactly jovial, he has a wry sense of humor. It could be that I was interpreting his reserve and more conventional style of dress – always collared shirts and slacks rather than jeans – as somber, rather than simply more formal than most men I knew.

After a minute of listening to the now-brown cornstalks swish softly in the breeze, I said, "You're pretty quiet this evening. You okay?"

Syl shifted in his chair but didn't look at me. "I moved to Southeast Iowa because I can run my business from anywhere. South County, sitting here along the river, looked peaceful." He paused for several seconds and grinned at me before turning his gaze back to the field. "And damn, if it isn't too quiet sometimes."

I waited a few seconds before replying. Syl had never said much about his life, and I didn't want to rush into a response. "Where you're from, near LA, right?"

He nodded.

"There's a lot of what I call passive activity in big cities. I mean, you can show up at a museum or park, heck even a big bookstore, and there'll be something going on. Here, if you want to feel part of something, you have to make friends. That gives you people to hang out with."

"You're my friend." He flashed a smile. "And Stooper, of course."

Stooper reinvented himself from town drunk to gardener when I asked him to help me with some of the heavier work at Syl's place. The two men have developed an unlikely friendship. For a while, I thought it was largely because Syl needed Stooper's help, but now I'm convinced they truly like each other. Syl even keeps a pitcher of iced tea in his fridge for Stooper.

"And I know I speak for Stooper when I say we're glad to know you. But if you want to talk to more people than us or Andy at the hardware store, you have to join something."

His brow furrowed. "You, uh, mean like a church?"

"You could, of course." I grinned. "You'd be a hit at any church social."

He grunted.

"But that's not what I meant. Our Lions and Rotary clubs aren't big, but you spend time with people doing something other than eating."

He laughed. "Your insurance guy, Bruce Blackner, he came by to see if I needed a different car insurance company. I didn't. He invited me to go to a Rotary lunch."

"Do it."

"You go?"

"I went when I was a reporter. I should rejoin. Now that I can live here without paying rent, I'm flush again."

Syl took the last pull on his beer and stood. "When's the next lunch?"

"Usually they meet the second and fourth Wednesday. I'll check and call you."

He reached for my empty beer bottle. "I live close enough to town to have a recycle bin."

I laughed. "You tree hugger, you."

He pointed a finger at me. "Conservationist, if you please."

Syl was almost to his truck when I called to him. "Farm Bureau annual meeting this Saturday. Tomorrow. You're my guest."

Since dusk had turned to night, I couldn't see his face, but his posture said he didn't think the Farm Bureau was his thing.

"A meeting?"

I laughed. "Basket dinner, short meeting. You'll meet fifty people."

"Oh, joy." He climbed into his truck. After he turned it around, he put down the window. "Should we invite Stooper?"

"Good call." I waved and turned toward the door. I bet if Syl still had friends in Los Angeles, they'd be surprised to hear he planned to spend Saturday evening hearing about the corn yield in South County, Iowa.

CHAPTER TWO

WHEN I CALLED STOOPER the next morning, Syl had already alerted him to the Saturday night plans.

"Can't quite see Syl mixing it up with the guys from the grain elevators," Stooper said.

"Some of them are the richest people in the county."

He shrugged. "Not all about money."

I almost said it is when you don't have much, but that wasn't the point. "I hear you. Syl's a businessman. The families at the Farm Bureau dinner are, too."

"What time?"

"The church social hall opens at five-thirty, dinner served about six."

Stooper grunted. "If Syl's going, I will. Some of those people won't be glad to see me."

I could imagine Stooper in his trademark blue jeans and flannel shirt cut off above the elbow. "Not a prom party. Besides, the only ones who saw you at Beer Rental Heaven will be glad to see you away from there."

"Dropped forty-four pounds since I stopped drinking. Joshua Marshall at the vet hospital lets me use the scale."

I laughed. "I'd never have the guts to weigh myself in a public place."

"You aren't fat."

"I'm five-six and sturdy."

He snorted. "See you at supper."

I hung up and called to tell the Farm Bureau secretary, who was also my neighbor Mrs. Donovan, that I was coming with two guests. I assured her I would bring lots of food.

"I can't believe I forgot you were the Farm Bureau secretary. Haven't you done that for maybe twenty-five years?"

"Twenty-three. I had hoped to make it to twenty-five, but Tom Dodson told me that when he becomes president in a year he has someone else in mind."

I could hear the disappointment in her voice. "Gosh, I'm sorry." I had no idea what else to say.

"I'll probably end up enjoying my leisure time. So, Melanie, I've already made copies of the materials to distribute. Can you and your guests share?"

"Of course." I gave her Syl and Stooper's names.

"I saw them having lunch at Mason's Diner the other day. And Stooper was eating a salad." She said the last word as if she had seen him eating a cutworm burger.

I smiled at the image of a burger made from the invasive corn crop pest. "He looks good, doesn't he?"

"Indeed. See you at five-thirty."

I tidied the kitchen and scrubbed its floor. As I got a bag of trash ready to carry to the burn barrel, my cell phone rang.

"Melody? Tom Dodson here."

Oh, good. He can't even get my name right. "Hello, Tom, long time no talk."

"I'm Farm Bureau vice-president this year, and I was just going over the attendance list with Mrs. Donovan. I've been meaning to call. Really glad you got clear title to your parents' farm."

When people said this, I had to quell irritation. When our late neighbor was trying to weasel it away from Ambrose and me, few people said they thought Frost's claims were bogus. I suppose they didn't want to take sides in case he won his outlandish court case. "Thanks much."

"So, since you're coming to Farm Bureau tonight, I wanted to nip some gossip in the bud."

"Okay... What's up, Tom?"

"You remember your dad was on the advisory group at my family's elevator?"

"Sure." As a kid, I called the local grain elevator "the silo place." I constantly asked to go inside the cylindrical, steel silos that contained the ground corn. Never was allowed in, of course.

"See, before his, uh, untimely death, your dad and I were kind of butting heads, but on crop stuff, not personally."

I said nothing for a few seconds. "I never heard him say a word. What did you disagree on?"

"Lots of discussion at the grain elevator about whether we should use the same equipment to grind GMO corn and regular corn. Your father and I came down on different sides of that."

"Sure, I heard Dad say he didn't like co-mingling, I think he called it. But he never mentioned you guys argued or anything."

"Like I said, it wasn't personal."

I had no idea where to go with the conversation, so I changed the subject. "I'll have to stop by the elevator sometime to talk about a contract for next year."

"Oh, sure. You aren't going to rent out the land anymore?"

"Not planning on it. I'll stop by after it's colder."

He cleared his throat. "Considerate of you. Always extra busy until a couple weeks after the first frost."

MISTER TIBBS AND I WENT into River's Edge to buy ingredients for banana bread and a spaghetti casserole my mom always took to the South County Farm Bureau dinner. I'm a surprisingly poor cook, considering I'm the daughter of a woman who regularly won blue ribbons for her pies at the county fair.

I prepared a mental shopping list as I drove through town, toward the Hy-Vee grocery. River's Edge is a community of 7,400, much of it spread along the Des Moines River about fifteen miles before it meanders into the Mississippi River in Missouri.

Some would say small-town living is boring, but I mostly don't. We have baseball diamonds and a soccer field, a town chorus that performs for free a few times a year, and an all-day Fourth of July celebration that starts with games in the morning and goes through fireworks. Plus the usual service clubs, town parades, and a huge annual street fair.

I passed Main Street, which leads to the small town square, the hub of River's Edge. It's no longer full of stores that sell things anyone really needs. People drive forty miles to Ottumwa or Mount Pleasant.

Mason's Diner, my regular hangout, is just off the square, which has antique stores, an artists' co-op, a bakery, coffee shop, things like that. If it weren't for Mr. Patel's variety store, there wouldn't even be a shop that sold sewing thread or baseball cards. Not that I bought either. You'd have to go to the very small pharmacy on one corner of the square and pay a lot for greeting cards and such.

As I inspected bananas to buy the most squishy, Sandi called to me from the other side of the Hy-Vee produce section. "Heard you're going to the dinner tonight."

I frowned at her. "I'm beginning to think my phone is bugged."

Her red ponytail shook as she laughed. "I was at the grain elevator earlier for a story I'm doing on grain separation. Tom Dodson mentioned he'd just spoken to you."

I moved toward her, bananas in hand. "Okay, I won't worry about spies on the phone lines."

She began to fill a sack with the small decorative gourds that populate part of the produce department every fall. "I guess he and your dad butted heads a lot. I didn't know that."

I wondered why Tom had mentioned that to her. "For some reason, Dad didn't want to use GMO seed. I always figured the higher cost made him avoid it."

Sandi shrugged. "Have you thought about what you'll use next spring?"

I started to tell her it might depend in part on what the farmers we leased to had planted, when she nearly squealed.

"You're buying spaghetti and grated cheese. Are you making your mom's casserole for tonight?"

"Yep. You going?"

"I'm covering it for the paper. Until just now I wasn't looking forward to it." Sandi grabbed a head of lettuce. "I better get there early. Unless you're making a double batch."

"I suppose I could." I glanced at my basket, calculating how much more I'd have to buy. "I have to hustle. Mister Tibbs and I have to stop at the hardware store on the way home."

"Getting some pumpkins?"

I shook my head. "Nope. I'm replacing the knobs on all the outside doors."

Sandi was just starting to shop, so I paid for my groceries and went outside to retrieve Mister Tibbs from her shady spot clipped to the bicycle rack. "Come on, girl. When we get to the hardware store you can come inside."

I INSPECTED A MIX OF deadbolts and doorknobs as Mister Tibbs strained on her leash. She wanted to go to our usual haunt, the gardening section. She likes the smells.

Andy's always-whiney voice came from behind me. "Finding what you need, Mel?"

I glanced at him. "Trying to decide if I want to go to the trouble of installing a deadbolt."

"You maybe got a drill. We sell a special piece for 'em, so's you can make the hole."

"Good to know." I didn't turn to fully face him. Andy is nosy and quick to pass gossip. I prefer to stay off his radar.

"You and Ambrose decided what you're doing with your farm?"

I turned toward him. "You mean like corn versus soybeans?"

He leaned his wiry frame against a shelf of nails and screws. It swayed gently, so he stood straight again. "I guess I mean are you sellin'?"

"Why would you even ask that? You know how hard Ambrose and I worked to keep it."

Andy's gaze shifted right, then left. "Just thought the people you rented to might offer to buy it. Or maybe keep farming it."

Ambrose had arranged the fairly simple contract that let the Kendig brothers and their wives use our fields. In exchange for no rental fee, we had split the profits fifty/fifty. Since our parents had owned the farm free and clear, we figured this would keep the land worked, while ownership was in dispute, and not put the Kendigs in the hole if corn was bringing in too little one year.

On the advice of our lawyer, we had put our share of any profits in an escrow account and didn't touch the money until ownership issues were resolved. I resented having had to skimp on everything when our money sat in the local bank.

"We have no intention to sell, Andy."

He nodded. "Which grain elevator you gonna use?"

"You're the second person to talk about grain elevators today. Are you asking everybody who comes in?"

"Not 'specially. Knew your old man and Dodson butted heads a lot."

I tuned out Andy, as I inspected doorknobs, and only picked up the end of his sentence.

"...fisticuffs at the last Farm Bureau meeting your dad was at."

I hung a doorknob back on its rack. "My father didn't get into 'fisticuffs' with anyone, Andy. Not for any reason."

Mister Tibbs didn't like missing a visit to the garden center, but if I kept talking to Andy, I would've thrown a doorknob at him.

CHAPTER THREE

AS I TOOK THE spaghetti casserole out of the oven, I wished I had not invited Syl and Stooper to the dinner this evening. Between Tom Dodson's call and Andy's comment about fisticuffs, I had begun to wonder if some people had been angry at my father. Not that it mattered now.

Syl's truck horn beeped once, and he turned off its engine. I glanced down to be sure no flour or a stray spaghetti noodle graced my black slacks or silver mock-turtleneck knit top.

Syl had insisted on driving. I thought he wanted to be sure he didn't walk into a room of strangers, if I arrived later than he did.

He knocked lightly on the side door, and I called, "It's open. You're in time to carry stuff out."

He walked into the kitchen and took in the older cabinetry and Formica flooring.

I grinned. "Think we have some updating to do?"

"I wasn't thinking that so much. This is the first time I've been in what I'd call a true farm kitchen. I like it. But..." He studied the cupboard in a corner. "Why does that cabinet have doors with metal squares with holes in the middle?"

I snapped the lid on the second casserole dish. "It's called a pie safe. Belonged to my grandmother. In the old days, you put pies and maybe bread in it to cool. Kept the bugs off stuff, and the holes let hot air escape."

"Huh. I'll chalk that up to another part of rural life I'm clueless about."

"I suppose air conditioning put the final nail in their coffins." I finished wrapping each casserole in a kitchen towel.

He nodded as he stacked the lidded casseroles to carry them out. "I guess punching holes in tin isn't much of a career option these days."

I grabbed the two wrapped loaves of banana bread and slung my purse over my shoulder. "We'd never sell it, but they used to bring a pretty penny. People aren't into antiques so much these days."

"Where did you keep it when you guys took all the furniture out of the house?"

"Ambrose and Sharon had what furniture we kept. They insisted the pie safe come back here. Kitchen would look pretty bare without it."

I glanced down as something wet touched my calf. "Mister Tibbs, you and your cold nose just went out. You'll be fine for a couple hours."

Mister Tibbs' eyes can implore without accompanying whining. I kept the purse on my shoulder, as I stooped to pat her white and beige ringlets. "Go to your spot. You can watch us leave."

"And come back," Syl added.

She emitted a barely audible growl.

"Hey, you like Syl."

"Still a strange house for her," he said.

I walked back to the kitchen and took a treat from the glass jar on the counter next to the fridge. Mister Tibbs trotted after me, tail wagging.

I tossed it a couple feet from me. "You scallywag. You planned that."

WHEN SYL AND I pulled into the Methodist Church parking lot, we spotted Stooper standing next to his battered Dodge Dart. Instead of jeans he wore a pair of corduroy pants that looked about ten years old, and a burgundy pullover sweater. I'd never seen him look so middle-class.

"What do you suppose got into Stooper?" I murmured.

Syl spoke quietly as he opened his door. "He drove over to the Goodwill store in Ottumwa to shop."

I slid out of the truck and turned to grab the bread. "Hey, Stooper, looking good."

He grinned as he walked to the truck bed to take one of the two casserole dishes. "New duds. I had the pants and shirt I wore to my father's funeral a few years ago, but they're way too big now."

"Congratulations," Syl said.

"Thanks. So, Mel, how much is this shindig?"

"It's free as long as you've paid your Farm Bureau dues and bring food. You're my guests."

We went into the church and walked down the flight of stairs to the basement community room.

"What if somebody can't do stairs?" Syl asked.

Elevator the size of a tin can kinda behind the pulpit area," Stooper said.

"Planning on losing more weight?" Syl asked.

I tried not to laugh. "God. I should have told you two you had to behave if I brought you."

Sandi's voice drifted down the steps. "Might work with Syl."

We had reached the bottom, and I saw Stooper grin at Syl before Syl asked Sandi, "What did you bring?"

Sandi took a large bag of round peppermint candies from her purse. "After dinner mints."

I raised my eyebrows at her. "Hot times in the kitchen?"

We turned right and entered the large community room with its cinderblock walls, indoor-outdoor carpet, and twenty or so round tables with chairs. I nodded toward the overflowing tables on the side of the huge room. "Guys, we'll head there to drop off our food."

"Our real food," Syl said.

As we placed the dishes on the table, Eliza Wright swooped over. "I'll put one in the oven to keep it warm." She gave Syl a dazzling smile. "And did you make this yourself, Hon?"

Syl balanced hot pads as he passed his dish to her. "I'm pretty good at scrambled eggs. That's about it. This is from Melanie."

Eliza's eyes widened briefly. As she walked away, she was undoubtedly internally debating whether Syl and I were dating. I don't think we are.

Stooper placed the casserole he had carried on the table and kind of grunted to Syl, "Notice she didn't ask me."

Syl and Stooper grinned at each other and surveyed the room, as I took the banana bread to the dessert end of the tables. I counted seven pies and several trays of brownies, plus a pile of cupcakes and a huge bowl of fruit. No one ever goes hungry at a Farm Bureau dinner.

Sandi sat her plastic bag of mints on the table near my bread. "Guess I should have brought a bowl."

A man's voice called, "Melanie."

Tom Dodson approached, right hand out to shake mine. "So good to see you again."

I took in his brown hair with more streaks of grey than I remembered. It had probably been a year since I'd seen him, and never in a suit.

I hadn't come the last two years. I didn't hibernate after my parents died, but I avoided some of the events we'd always done together, like Farm Bureau and the local craft fairs my mother loved. "Thanks, Tom." I extended my hand and shook his.

He nodded at Sandi and got right to his point, a frown firmly in place. "Now Bernard Hopewell might come over to try to get you to switch to his elevator. But you'd have to drive an extra couple miles, and that's a lot of gas with a big load."

I couldn't put a finger on it, but something about Tom Dodson had begun to annoy me. The man had barely spoken to me in years, and I didn't remember him coming to my parents' funeral. Not that I remembered everyone who came. It was so huge the minister had asked someone to create an Internet feed for those who had to sit in this very community room.

I withdrew my hand, but smiled. "Ambrose and I have a lot to talk about. I don't imagine we'll do things differently than Mom and Dad."

Bruce Blackner cleared his throat.

Saved by the cough. "Hey, Bruce. Good to see you."

Anyone can join Farm Bureau, so nearly all the non-agricultural business owners in town did. I suspected half the reason was to make sure they had a shot at getting the members' business for insurance or hairstyling or whatever.

Bruce turned to Tom. "Now, Tom, don't scare Melanie away."

Tom's smile was tight-lipped. "Just welcoming her back."

"Thanks, Tom," I said.

Sandi's eyes met mine and looked away, as Tom kind of stomped off.

I returned my gaze to Bruce. "How's my favorite insurance seller?"

He grinned. "I should have used my phone to record that." He lowered his voice. "Give me a buzz on Monday."

Mr. Patel called to Bruce, and he walked away.

As I glanced toward Mr. Patel, I noted Brenda Chase stop Tom Dodson, as she pointed to a clipboard she carried. Brenda's a year older than my twenty-nine years and recently divorced. Rumor has it she's on the prowl for a boyfriend. Tom's huge smile, as he seemed to answer a question, made me wonder if she'd found one.

Syl and Stooper came over, and the four of us moved a few feet away from the serving table.

Stooper stared after Bruce. "You in the market for some insurance stuff?"

"Not particularly," I said.

Brenda and her clipboard approached us. "Hello, you three."

Stooper stiffened.

I smiled. "Syl, Stooper, and I did reserve together."

Stooper relaxed. I figured he had thought she meant Sandi, Syl and me, thus ignoring him.

Brenda faltered, but only for a second. "Two years ago, we began assigning people to specific tables. That way there's a good mix of conversation."

"Oh?" Syl asked.

Brenda directed her brilliant smile to him. "Now we have you at Table Three. It'll give you a chance to meet a nice cross-section of people. You do keep to yourself, Mr. Seaton."

"Syl," he said, and he followed her nod to the other side of the room. Table Three was larger than most others. I glimpsed the mayor and high school principal, before Brenda took Syl's arm and blocked my view as she guided him away.

He turned his head to throw me a dirty look – or maybe it was desperation – as he let her steer him away.

I turned to Stooper and Sandi. "I hope we're together."

"If we aren't, I'm headin' out," Stooper said.

Before I could say we could likely rearrange, Sandi said, "There's a seating chart at the sign-in table. You bypassed it when you took your food to the serving table. You two are together."

"Whew," Stooper said, grinning. "I really wanted some of that grub."

Sandi laughed. "I'm where they always stick reporters, at the far table." She nodded to the back of the room. "But if someone doesn't show up at your table, I'll move over."

She gestured with her head to indicate that Stooper and I should move a few feet closer to the painted cinderblock wall. We followed.

"So, Mel." She lowered her voice and took in Stooper with a nod. "The big reason they started assigning seats was because three years ago a couple people almost got into a fight."

"Here?" Stooper asked. "What, over the last piece of pie?"

Sandi grinned. "I wish. About a new pesticide that somebody used, and whether some of it drifted over to one of the farms that does organic produce."

I frowned. "I don't remember that."

Stooper nodded. "Kind of in the parking lot. You probably already left to write your story."

Sandi shrugged. "Your article that year had bunches of pictures, and you wanted to work on the layout."

"I know, two years before I left the paper."

"You mean got canned," Stooper said. "Best thing that ever happened to me."

Sandi stared at him until he grinned.

"A motivated gardener," I said, wanting to be sure she knew I was used to Stooper's sometimes odd humor.

Sandi glanced around the room. "Just don't bring up pesticides, genetically modified seed, or which grain elevator pays more attention to that."

I blew out a breath. "Okay, I know what conversations to avoid."

"Uh, one more thing," Sandi said. "The people who were most heated were some friends of your father's, people who had banded together to take their business from Dodson's elevator to another one. Hopewell's place, I think."

In the months before he died, my Father had begun to come into town more, often meeting a few other farmers at Mason's Diner. A couple times they drove over to Keosauqua. He had said they were trying out a new greasy spoon, as he put it. Had he been avoiding some people he disagreed with?

A waving arm caught my attention, and I raised a hand to Mr. Patel. Odd, he didn't usually pay much attention to me. My gaze crossed Tom Dodson's, and he wore a deep scowl.

I smiled and turned back to Sandi and Stooper. "Too much intrigue for me. Let's get seated."

Stooper frowned. "Too bad we can't hang out here and be first in line."

AS THE AFTER-DINNER presentations wound down, I remembered why I had not liked being assigned to cover these dinners for the paper. Too much to pay attention to on a full stomach.

Stooper had his elbow on the table and rested his head on his raised fist. Every now and then his eyes closed and he swayed for a second before he reopened them. I grinned at him, when he looked up after one of his larger sways.

He sat up straighter.

I leaned toward him. "I have to go to the ladies' room for a second."

"Traitor," he mumbled.

The restrooms were in the hallway, and the door leading out of the community room was not far from our table. I glanced at Table Three as I walked. The high school principal sat next to Syl, so close that her shoulder almost touched his. *I wonder who engineered that?*

When I finished using the facilities, I splashed water on my face. Makeup be damned this late in the evening.

I looked left and right, as I reemerged into the hallway. A motion to my right caught my eye. A deep, open coat closet off the hallway had few jackets since it was still fairly warm. The motion came again.

I walked down the hallway and looked into the closet. A man lay sprawled on the floor.

"Oh, my," I yelled, as I approached him. "Call 9-1-1." Since he had moved, I felt somewhat calm as I knelt beside him.

As voices rose behind me, Tom Dodson's bloody hand reached toward me. He grabbed my knit shirt at stomach level, and the grip helped him pull his head a couple of inches off the floor.

"Be still, Tom. Help's coming."

What on earth could have caused the blood? Was he on blood thinners and a small cut bled freely?

His head thudded to the floor, obviously involuntarily. His open and unseeing eyes stared blankly into mine.

CHAPTER FOUR

FROM BEHIND ME, SANDI'S was the first voice that came through clearly. "My God, Mel, what the hell?"

Even though stunned, the combination of God and hell in the same sentence almost struck me funny. "I…I don't know."

"Move aside, Melanie."

I recognized Doc Shelton's voice. He'd been my family doctor since I was a child, and his presence calmed me. Still squatting, I almost tumbled to my left as he knelt beside me.

Shocked murmurs came from behind us. A woman said, "Call an ambulance," countered by a man's voice that said, "Call the sheriff."

Someone flipped a switch, and the dark closet became awash in flickering fluorescent lighting. The buzz added to the confusion in my head.

Doc Shelton deftly ran his fingers over the back of Dodson's head, and they came away bloody.

Behind us, a woman's voice screamed, "Tom! What happened?"

I reached for the wall as I stood, not certain I could stay on my feet without assistance. Someone took my elbow, and I met Sandi's wide eyes, as she pulled me back a couple of feet.

Tom Dodson's wife knelt beside Doc Shelton.

He appeared almost as stunned as she was. "Janet, now Janet, I don't believe we can…"

She began to wail. "No!"

Sandi dragged me back a few more feet, as Bruce Blackner nudged by and knelt next to Janet Dodson. "Come away, Janet. Let me help you."

The wail turned to a moan, and she said, "It can't be. Everything was just getting better."

I had a second to register that I didn't know what had been bad, before she half-turned to look at me. "What did you do?"

"I found him. I'm so sorry." My nose began to run, and I sniffed loudly.

"Don't you pretend to cry, Melanie Perkins. You did this!"

Several people said things like, "Janet, no" or "Janet, you're upset."

A stronger hand took hold of my shoulder and tugged, and I almost fell into Syl. "Come away, Melanie."

I consider myself pretty tough, but finding a body, especially so soon after I had talked to the person, had me numb. I let Syl and Sandi walk me through the now packed hallway back into the community room.

Since several people seemed to stare at my chest, I looked down. A couple of Tom Dodson's bloody fingerprints clashed with my silver top. *Ugh.*

The three of us reached Stooper, who stood next to the table where he and I had eaten. I wondered for a moment why he hadn't come to the hall, and then I realized my purse sat in the chair I'd used. My guess was he didn't want to leave it, and I almost giggled at the thought of Stooper carrying it to find me.

Syl pointed to a chair, and I sat, kind of sideways.

Sandi sat next to me. "What happened?"

"Fill us in, Melanie," Syl said.

"I'm not sure. When I came out of the ladies' room, a motion in the coat area caught my eye." I swallowed and reached for a glass of water and sipped. Half of it ran down my chin. "When I walked over, I saw someone."

"Who?" Stooper asked.

"Tom Dodson," Sandi said.

"Crud," Stooper said.

Syl looked at him.

"Him and Mel's father argued about some stuff."

"But what would that matter?" I asked. "Anyway, I walked over and saw a person on the floor, and I knelt down and yelled someone should call 9-1-1."

"So, he was alive?" Sandi asked.

I thought for a second. "For a moment. I'm, uh, not sure. Oh. Yes." I pointed to my shirt. "He reached up to me, just for a second."

Sandi's eyes widened, and she looked away.

Janet Dodson's sobs had grown more distant. Bruce Blackner or someone had apparently moved her away from the closet, not in the direction of the community room. I felt bad for her, but I didn't want to be publicly accused of killing her husband. At least, not more than she had already.

People drifted back into the room. My gaze went to Eliza Wright, as she put lids on dishes on the serving table. Her pursed lips and stiff movements said she was well aware of what was going on. I supposed she wanted to stay busy.

Syl sat next to Sandi and nodded at me. "Sheriff or somebody's going to want to talk to you."

"No kiddin'," Stooper said.

I looked up at him. "Do you remember how long I was gone? I think it was just a couple of minutes."

"Five at most," Syl said. "I saw you leave."

Sandi nodded. "Surely, no one will think..." She stopped when I raised my eyebrows at her.

"Melanie!" Sheriff Gallagher called from the doorway. "Stick around, please."

I raised my voice. "Of course."

He turned to go back to Dodson's body. Or I assumed that's where he'd go. Maybe he had people searching the building.

"You okay, Mel?" Stooper asked.

"Not really. Better than Tom."

Sandi took a small notebook from her purse. "Sorry, Mel, I have to ask."

"You won't really need to take notes. There's nothing else to tell."

She nodded, but didn't put the pad away. "You didn't see anyone else?"

"Nope. Not a soul. Do you know anyone who was mad at him?"

She shook her head. "No more than usual. He wasn't known to be patient."

"And he didn't cut people a lot of slack on their bills," Stooper said.

Syl looked around Sandi to Stooper. "How do you know he didn't just fall and hit his head? Bills for what?"

"Grain elevator stuff," Stooper said. "Hopewell, at the other elevator, gives people more of a chance to get paid for their corn before they pay him."

I wished I could remember any conversations, in which my dad talked about Dodson.

Syl shrugged. "I only give my clients two weeks."

I took another sip of water. This time it stayed off my chin. "Yes, but they have money when they hire you."

"Mostly," he smiled.

Stooper finally sat down. "Some farmers don't have it 'til they complete their contracts. You know, for sales."

In a low voice, Sandi said, "Here comes trouble."

Sheriff Gallagher nearly growled, "You think my hearing's bad?"

Sandi flushed. "Sorry."

Gallagher took a chair from the table next to ours, swung it around, and faced me. "What can you tell me, Melanie?"

Sheriff Gallagher is a large man, whom I know to be fair. And gruff. "There's not much to tell." I recounted seeing a motion in the opening to the coat closet, and finding Dodson.

"When's the last time you saw him?"

"Sheriff, come on," Syl began.

He held up one hand. "I see Tom's prints on Mel, but no blood spatter on her. Everything is pertinent at this point." He turned his gaze to me. "Afraid I'm going to need your shirt, Melanie."

I looked down at Tom Dodson's prints. Since I'd ridden with Syl, I didn't have a spare shirt or sweater, which I usually have in my truck bed.

"I, uh, have a sweatshirt in my trunk," Sandi said.

I nodded. "So, Sheriff, Tom came over to me when we first got here. He said he hoped Ambrose and I would work with his elevator, like Dad did. Before that..." I thought for a couple of seconds. "I called to make a reservation for tonight, and he heard and called me back."

Gallagher took in Syl, Stooper, and Sandi. "So, you three are 'we.'"

I shook my head. "Stooper, Syl, and I came together."

"The three S's," Sandi murmured.

I smiled at Gallagher's momentary confusion. "She's a word person."

He grunted. "Why'd he call after you made the reservation?"

I shrugged. "He was going over the list with Mrs. Donovan. I hadn't been here the last two years, so that'd be a total of three years ago. He said he and Dad had words about some things, but it wasn't personal. I had no idea what he was talking about."

Gallagher expelled a breath. "Damn."

"What?" I asked.

"Could be some sort of motive," Sandi said.

My sarcasm came through. "Oh, sure. I'm so mad about something I never heard of that I secreted a weapon and hit him on the head?"

Eliza Wright's voice was high-pitched. "You did?"

Syl and Stooper said, "No, she didn't."

Gallagher added, "You about through puttin' food away, Eliza?"

When she stomped into the nearby kitchen, he regarded me with narrowed eyes. "How'd you know he got hit in the head?"

"Doc Shelton put his hand behind Dodson's head, and it came away, came away…bloody."

Sandi handed me my water glass.

"Sorry." Not all that long ago, Ambrose and I had come across a body in our barn. I didn't like those memories and didn't want more.

Gallagher stood. "This motion you saw. It was Dodson?"

"I suppose. What else could it have been?"

Deputy Newt Harmon, in his early twenties and the youngest of the sheriff's small staff, spoke from the entrance to the room. "Sheriff? The medical examiner's here."

Gallagher had the slightest trace of a smile, as he said, "Call me if you're leaving South County." He stood and walked toward Newt.

The four of us were silent for several seconds, until Syl spoke. "At least, he didn't say don't leave town."

I drained my glass. I'd need the restroom again soon. No way I'd walk into the restroom near Dodson's body. As I thought this, more people came back into the community room, presumably to get their purses and leftovers and such.

"Do you suppose we can go?" The tiny elevator sat in a back hallway, and I preferred that option for an exit.

Sandi picked up her purse, as we all stood. "Mel, I need to go through the crowd, to see what I can pick up. But I'll hurry, so I can bring you my sweatshirt."

I glanced at my top and suppressed a shudder. "Story of the year."

She flushed.

"I didn't mean it to sound snarky," I said.

Stooper squared his shoulders. "I'll walk out with Sandi in case she needs muscle gettin' out."

"Good idea." I avoided Sandi's eyes, which I knew would be rolling.

Syl and I picked up my empty casserole dishes from the serving table and I fastened the lids on them. I glanced around. Where would I change into Sandi's sweatshirt?

Eliza Wright, looking all of her eighty-plus years, came out of the kitchen and spoke quietly. "I heard the sheriff say you'd have to leave your shirt. You can change real quick in that big food cupboard. The door shuts."

"Thanks." I busied myself by picking up used napkins from a couple of tables and putting them in a trash can. Syl did the same, and the few people who had come back into the room ignored us.

Sandi came back at a trot and almost tossed me the sweatshirt, before turning to leave again. "I'll stop by the farm in a bit."

As she left, Newt Harmon scanned the room, saw me and came over. "Mel, sheriff said..."

"Yeah, I'm going to change now." I held up Sandi's sweatshirt. "Okay if I put my top in a clean garbage bag from the kitchen?"

He nodded, and I thought his look held sympathy. "Take your time."

I took less than a minute to change and return to hand him the bag. He and Syl had been talking quietly and stopped when I walked up.

"Thanks, Melanie," Newt said, and walked out, bag in hand.

Syl and I walked in silence toward the elevator. Then he said, "If Stooper's muscle, what am I?"

"A good friend."

CHAPTER FIVE

I WOKE UP SUNDAY MORNING with a decided headache and lay staring at the ceiling. I'm always good for a couple of beers, but three after ten o'clock at night had not set well with my stomach or head.

Stooper, Syl, and I had sat on the farmhouse side porch for twenty minutes before Sandi joined us. She brought a twelve-pack of seltzer water, which was great for Stooper. I had only myself to blame for the beer.

What Sandi hadn't brought was meaningful news about what had happened to Tom Dodson. She did say people were annoyed that they weren't able to leave until the sheriff or a deputy talked to each of them. I bet that had taken a while.

Mister Tibbs isn't allowed to sleep in my bed, but she does gently tug on the bedspread when I linger in the sack longer than she deems appropriate. I never want to ignore her bladder.

The temperature was too warm for frost, and the sun had burned off the morning dew. With me still in sleeping pants and a sweatshirt over my tee-shirt, we toured the yard and trotted around the barn.

Except we didn't go at our usual pace. Mister Tibbs would only go as fast as a walk. I figured she hadn't slept much either.

.As we approached the house, my former colleague Ryan drove up in the *South County News'* red Ford Focus.

Ryan and I have barely spoken the last few months. I considered his coverage of our neighbor's murder to be very unfair, and he said he was being 'unbiased.' Sandi said she thinks we should agree to disagree. I agreed to disagree with her.

He had the decency to look uncomfortable.

"Mel, you doing okay?"

Mister Tibbs ran to him and did some serious smelling of his shoes as he shut the car door.

"I'm fine, Ryan. What do you want?"

"Scott assigned me to cover the story. Can I talk to you?"

The *South County News* Advisory Board, which Doc Shelton heads, appointed Scott Holmes acting editor after Hal's death. I'd been offered the interim position and declined. Though that might be why I don't like Scott's somewhat intense approach – for a small-town paper – I don't think that's it. I look forward to the board picking Hal's permanent replacement. The application deadline was at least a couple of weeks ago.

I made no move to invite him into the house. "Sure. Did Sandi fill you in?"

"Come on, Mel. You can't still be pissed."

I didn't smile. "You reported on Peter Frost's murder the way your boss thought it should go. That approach might work at his former paper in Iowa City, but you only put in one side of the story."

He flushed. "Look, I'm sorry, okay?"

I narrowed my eyes. Ryan is in his early twenties and determined to make it to a major daily. He's smart, but I don't think cutting corners will get him there. "If I thought that was a genuine apology, I'd accept it. You just want me to talk to you."

He tapped the slim reporter's notebook against one thigh. "I could say you refused to talk to me."

"You know what? Go ahead. Tell Scott if he wants an interview he can come out here himself."

It hadn't rained for a couple of weeks, so the Focus kicked up dust as Ryan made a three-point turn to get back on the gravel road.

THE HOUSE PHONE RANG AS I finished getting dressed half-an-hour later. "Good morning."

Janet Dodson's tone was clipped. "Not exactly."

I said nothing, then managed, "I'm so sorry about Tom."

She took a breath. "Look, the sheriff has explained that you couldn't possibly have killed Tom. I'm sorry for what I said last night."

"You don't need to apologize. I get why it could have looked that way to you."

Now she said nothing.

"You have, uh, adult children, don't you?"

"Yes, my daughter is in Lincoln. She'll get in early tomorrow."

"Can I do something for you? Make a casserole in case you have a lot of people over?" *Why did I offer that? I don't want to go to her house.*

Her tone softened. "Thanks, but the neighbors have brought over enough food to feed half the town. Sylvia at the beauty shop called to say I'd feel better with a fresh wash and set, so I'm heading over there in a few minutes."

"Really nice of her to go in on a Sunday. Please call if I can help you in some way."

In her clipped tone, she thanked me and hung up.

I didn't get why she was so short with me, but I hadn't just lost a husband.

I rinsed out the beer bottles and put them into a plastic sack to take to the recycling bin in town. Why would anyone kill Tom Dodson? I didn't buy the GMO/non-GMO arguments. Sure, with the right or wrong people, any discussion can turn angry, even violent.

But the Farm Bureau meeting wasn't a place people brought weapons...wait. I didn't even know whether Tom had been hit on the head or shot. Surely a shot would have reverberated around the building.

Everything came back to why someone hit him. Was it to intentionally kill or simply lash out in anger? Janet Dodson had said things were just getting better. Better than what?

My cell phone buzzed. Sandi. I opened with, "Bet I know what you want."

"Melanie, why wouldn't you talk to Ryan?"

"Don't trust him. He wants to sensationalize whatever happened last night."

She had an edge to her voice. "You don't know that."

"Not willing to find out otherwise. How come you didn't come? You were there."

She was silent for several seconds. "Scott thinks I might be too close to it."

"Don't you mean too close to me?"

"That might be what he meant, but it's not what he said."

"I told Ryan to tell Scott he could call me anytime."

"You get me."

"Is he chicken?" I asked.

"No, just annoyed. You have anything to add to what we talked about last night?"

I started to mention Janet's call, but that seemed private. Besides, Janet could speak for herself. "Nope. You know what I did when we left the meeting."

"I do."

"Did you hear anything?"

"Not really. Sheriff made it clear he has no reason to suspect you."

"Thanks for the loan of the sweatshirt, by the way."

"Sure. You had breakfast? Want to meet at the diner?"

"Just coffee. The diner beats cold cereal. I'll get Mister Tibbs settled and meet you there in twenty."

ON A MORNNG when I felt out of sorts, I appreciated the familiarity of Mason's Diner's booths, counter serving space, and linoleum floor. And its brassy waitress.

Shirley's voice came across the diner as soon as I walked in. "Shug, what are you up to?"

When I want to know something, I find Shirley. She has her ears open all the time, but she doesn't have the mean edge that Eliza Wright can. Or Andy. "Staying out of trouble."

She stood, a hand on each hip of her mustard-colored food server uniform. "Not what I'm hearing."

I spotted Sandi at a booth toward the back of the narrow diner. "Shirley, it's Sunday. Why are you here?"

"I'm gettin' a perm Monday, so I traded. Coffee with sugar and half a toasted bagel?"

I grinned, nodded, and started for Sandi. I slid into the red vinyl booth across from her. "Hear much in the last half-hour?"

She drank her tomato juice. "Somebody started a collection for Tom's funeral."

"They own the elevator. Don't they have money?"

She shrugged. "Corn prices are down some. I don't know if he's been charging less or if people are slow paying."

"Come on, he's close to sixty. He never saved anything?"

"I know, weird." She took a bite of her oatmeal.

Sandi's breakfast choice – oatmeal and tomato juice – has always turned my stomach. More so today, with the beer still roiling. "And doesn't Janet teach or something?"

"Secretary at the middle school."

Shirley plopped my coffee and bagel in front of me. "What I heard is he let his life insurance policy run out."

I stared at her. "Glad I have mine on auto pay from my checking account."

She turned back toward the kitchen. "Rates get pretty pricey when you get old, Shug."

Sandi shrugged and lowered her voice. "Not having even a few thousand dollars, that sounds like somebody with a sick kid or a lot of debt. As far as I know, their grandkids are healthy."

"And you don't cancel your insurance when you get older. Cut the amount to lower premiums, maybe." I remembered Bruce Blackner had told me to call him Monday. I'd forgotten all about that. What did he want?

"What?" Sandi asked.

I shook my head slowly. "Doesn't make sense. The recession's been over for years. Did he gamble, you think?"

"It's not the 1950s. Everybody does."

"You know what I mean. Visit the casinos a lot."

"Or drugs," she said. "Maybe he bought a lot of pills or something."

"Gee. Listen to us. Me, especially. I just got through a couple of bad years."

"Sure, but that was because Peter Frost was trying to screw you and Ambrose. We're looking for some reason a guy Dodson's age wouldn't have enough to pay for his funeral."

AS I INSTALLED NEW exterior doorknobs, which I had finally bought at the hardware store that afternoon, I thought about my parents.

They were savers. Even when I made little, I always saved something. Of course, any agricultural business had fluctuating profits – and losses. But most farmers kept business and family finances separate. That way, you could literally lose the farm, but not your house or personal savings.

Other than caring about anyone in town who died, I had no reason to mourn Tom Dodson. If he had not called to say he and my dad had argued, my interest would have been the same as anyone else's in town. Who in the heck would murder someone at a Farm Bureau meeting in a church basement?

Dodson said Dad was on the elevator's advisory board. I didn't pay much attention to his various committees, but he must have had some files.

My memory skimmed through the painful first three months after our parents were killed in that fiery crash on an icy December night. When Peter Frost claimed to have some notes and a verbal contract to buy the farm for a low price, Ambrose's and my attorney, Ken Brownberg, had advised us to move Mom and Dad's belongings out of the house.

We'd sold some bulky items and Ambrose had found a friend willing to store the tractor and combine. But what about the contents of Dad's home office?

"Damn!" As I picked up my phone to call Ambrose, I realized I should have let him know about me being found next to Dodson's body. He always says I don't tell him when I'm in trouble.

I walked to the porch as I dialed, and when he answered, I said, "Happy Sunday, brother."

"I wondered how long it would take you to call me. Sharon said it would be today, so she wins our bet."

I smiled. "What was the bet?"

"She wants me to get rid of my goats."

That made me laugh outright. Ambrose mostly has them to provide milk to some group that helps families whose kids are allergic to cow's milk. Last April, they ate all of Sharon's tulips. "But they're so cute."

Ambrose must have put me on speaker phone, because Sharon called out, "They also get out of their pen and poop all over the place."

I avoided asking if they fertilized the vegetable garden she grew behind their farmhouse. "Nobody suspects me of anything. But it was a terrible experience."

Ambrose's tone softened. "All I heard was you found Tom Dodson on the floor in the Methodist Church community room."

"The coat closet down the hall." I described what had happened, avoiding mention of Tom's bloody fingerprints on my shirt. "I feel sorry for Janet Dodson, you know, being right there when it happened."

"I'm so glad you were with friends," Sharon said.

"Me, too. I also wanted to ask you about Dad arguing with Dodson about GMO issues."

Ambrose's tone hardened. "What did you hear?"

I didn't mention Andy's fisticuffs comment, but filled him in, basically repeating what Sandi had told me.

Ambrose sighed. "Dad opposed any use of GMO seed, but I think he was more hacked off because he thought Dodson was jacking up prices."

"Why didn't I know that?"

I could almost see Ambrose shrug. "You lived there, so you did a lot with Mom and Dad. But he and I talked crops. I told him I thought eventually the GMO stuff would be a non-issue, and suggested he switch to Hopewell's elevator. He didn't like my opinion, but we didn't argue."

"So, this advisory board he was on. What was that?"

"Publicity thing for Dodson, mostly, I think. Family business doesn't need a board, but I guess it was a way to keep farmers involved, so they'd use his elevator."

"Did Dad talk to you about it?"

Ambrose said nothing for several seconds. "Melanie, I think it would look funny for you to poke around about Dodson. Not like you work at the paper anymore."

"Sandi's writing about it."

"Leave it to Sandi."

"I hear you." But I didn't say I'd leave it to her. I had no intention of investigating anything, but any person who watched someone die would want to know why it happened.

CHAPTER SIX

SINCE AMBROSE PROBABLY WOULDN'T tell me if Dad and Tom Dodson fought a lot, I reverted to my mental ruminations about what we had done with Mom and Dad's personal stuff beyond getting rid of a bunch of furniture and clothes and such.

We'd donated a lot of kitchen items to the Red Cross, when another family had a house fire. I kept Mom's big kitchen mixer, in case I ever decided to really learn to cook.

But what about paperwork? I knew we gave some documents about the farm deed to our lawyer, but Dad had a file cabinet. Did I box up those files? Every part of me had been numb for weeks after their deaths. Would I remember if I did?

From my chair on the side porch, I stared into the cornfield. Mister Tibbs had been curled in a ball in her doggie bed. She'd awakened and stared at me as I talked to Ambrose, but seemed to know I wouldn't pet her when I was talking. Now, she stretched and came over.

I leaned over to pet her. "I didn't have you then, so you can't help me think."

She plopped down and put her head on my foot. Then it came to me. Mrs. Donovan had insisted on helping. I'd demurred a couple of times, but she did help one day, and I trusted her enough to let her pack the file cabinet and stuff from Dad's desk. I called her.

I listened politely as she said she was sorry about my finding Tom Dodson, and we said we felt bad for Janet. Then I asked my question.

"Well now, Melanie, I'm not one-hundred percent sure, but I remember you put them into your truck. Would Hal have let you store them at the paper?"

"I don't..." The image of the boxes in the back of my pickup jarred my memory. "You know, I think Mrs. Keyser let me put them in her attic."

"Well now, that would have been right kind of her," Mrs. Donovan said.

I thanked her and hung up. My former landlady had been sorry to lose my monthly rent in the house we shared. To ensure my solvency after I lost my job at the paper, she found me my second landscaping client, Dr. Carver, who had just moved to town.

While a perfectly good landlord, Mrs. Keyser was nosy. I grabbed a sweater from the hook by the back door and hoped I had taped the boxes shut.

I OFTEN HAD TO PINCH myself not to laugh at Mrs. Keyser's housedresses. Today's had kittens in shades of pink and green, a bright blue yarn ball between them. Seams didn't line up, so it was more like a ball with a split personality.

She led me into her portion of her two-unit house in town. "It's nice to see you, Melanie. My, I miss having you upstairs."

I accepted the proffered spot on an old-fashioned loveseat. "Smells as if you're baking something. I miss those smells."

"I don't eat too many of the cookies I bake. I mostly put them in the freezer in case I need to take them to cards or bingo."

"Did you get any responses to your ad to rent the apartment?"

"I've had a few calls. I'd rather have someone I know, and I want someone quiet."

"I'll ask around." And I would. "Can they have small pets?"

As I asked this, her cat hopped onto the loveseat beside me. I realized the cloth placemat on the other couch cushion was for her. She began to smell me vigorously, probably recognizing Mr. Tibbs' scent.

Mrs. Keyser sighed. "I've been saying cats only though, of course, I'd prefer none."

I got to the reason for my visit. "So, Mrs. Keyser, my brain was a bit muddled for a while after my folks' car accident. Did I put some boxes in your attic?"

"My lands, you did. My daughter says I can't go up there alone anymore." Her eyes brightened. "You're here. How about if we both go up? I've been looking for a tea set that belonged to my mother. I'm sure it's up there."

Fortunately, entry to her attic was by narrow stairs rather than a ladder. Much easier to carry down my heavy file boxes and several of her crates of Christmas decorations and "family memories."

After promising I would stop by in a few days to carry some things back to her attic, I began to drive home. I changed my mind and drove west, toward Syl's five acres on the edge of town. He wasn't likely to be in Des Moines on a Sunday afternoon.

I pulled into Syl's driveway and studied his home, a center hall colonial that has had a couple of additions. I'm partial to his well-landscaped yard, and he's had the interior repainted in shades darker than I've ever used, plus white baseboards. Even the floors have been refinished. If you didn't know he was on the edge of a small town, you'd think you were in a city house.

Syl must have heard my truck, because he came out his side door and waved. I climbed out of the truck and walked toward him. "Just picked up some boxes at Mrs. Keyser's and thought I'd stop by."

"Come on in. You just missed Stooper. He's worried about you."

Syl's side door opens into a large kitchen, which has a formal dining room to one side and a front foyer between it and the living room. I followed him into the living room and we sat in two of the several Queen Ann chairs grouped in front of the fireplace.

"I'm okay. I even remembered to call Ambrose."

He smiled. "Before he called you?"

I grinned back. "Yes, but he'd already heard." I sobered. "Couple people have told me my dad and Tom Dodson butted heads about some issues at the elevator. I didn't know that, but it made sense that Ambrose would."

After I explained the few things I'd heard, including Andy's snarky questions, Syl stared into his fireplace. "Of course, his disagreements with your father were years ago, but it's an odd coincidence that Dodson talked to you about them not long before he died."

I nodded. "I thought he was being…ingratiating. Anyway, Sheriff Gallagher doesn't suspect me, but some people in River's Edge thrive on gossip."

He shrugged. "Nothing you can do about that."

"True, but I remembered where some of my dad's old files were. Mrs. Keyser let me store some in her attic. I just picked them up. I want to see if he had any records of what he did with Dodson's advisory board."

Syl's eyebrows went up. "If it's not confidential stuff, I could go through some of the business papers with you. Unless you think Ambrose wouldn't like that."

Ambrose didn't know Syl well, but he liked him. "It'll be okay. I should know what's in those boxes anyway."

"You want to carry a couple boxes in now? You don't have a big table yet."

"I hadn't thought about that. Sure."

We brought in the two boxes labeled file drawers, and we each opened one. I hadn't taped them and wondered if we'd be the first to search them. Not that Mrs. Keyser would have taken anything.

Syl began making a methodical list of all the file names while I quickly went through folders about utility bills and crop insurance. Finally, I came to two thick ones, both labeled ***Dodson Elevator***.

"Here we go." I shrugged at Syl. "I have no idea what we're looking for."

"Always go for the money."

I could interpret profit and loss statements, but I wouldn't be able to tell if something other than the math was suspicious. "Sure." I quickly thumbed through both files. "They're organized chronologically."

I passed him the older one, which started two years before my dad died, and I took the one that covered his last year on the advisory board. I started by reading the minutes.

At early meetings that year, an elderly farmer named Jeb Nelson was the recording secretary. His minutes were fairly detailed. No discussion of GMO seed, despite what Dodson had told me. The notes for April and May discussed the possibility of the elevator becoming a co-op. Dad and several others liked this idea, since prices for grain drying and storage had been going up substantially.

I couldn't imagine why Dodson would essentially sell his business. Dad had alluded to the fact that there didn't appear to be a family successor. Mr. Donovan was also on the board, and he suggested Tom and Janet could retire in style.

After May, Janet Dodson began doing the minutes, and they dropped from three or four pages that described discussion to single-page notes that simply relayed topics and decisions made, if any. Purchase a larger ad in the Farm Bureau newsletter, repair a piece of drying equipment. Literally dry notes.

Syl cleared his throat. "See anything interesting?"

I looked up. "Seems my father was among those advocating that Dodson consider selling the elevator, so it could become a co-op."

"Huh. Were profits down?"

"I've been reading minutes, not attachments to them."

He gestured I should hand him the documents.

I slid my file to him and took his. "From the tone of the last notes Jeb Nelson took, Dodson was very opposed to the idea."

Syl shrugged. "I wouldn't sell my consulting business just because others thought it a good idea."

"Of course not. But I would've thought he'd jump at the idea to make at least a couple million and get out of the daily grind."

Syl's eyebrows went up. "He actually had an offer?"

I shook my head. "That's my guess about value. At the last meeting with detailed notes, a couple people asked him if he would be willing to hold a note or if he'd want all financing done through a bank. He said the discussion was closed, and Janet Dodson became the recording secretary after that."

"So, no discussion of it?"

"If there was, she didn't write it down."

Syl pulled several end-of-year financial statements from the two files and put them side-by-side. "Looks as if your father had statements from a couple years before he joined the group, plus the three years he was on it."

I went to the other side of his large dining table, so I could look at the reports right side up.

Syl began to mark each year's net profit with a pencil checkmark. When he was done, he asked, "Tell me what you think of these bottom-line numbers."

I studied them. Profits had stayed almost steady for the years Dad served on the committee. The prior two years they had gone up slightly. "I'd have to look at corn and bean prices, but I'd say making a clear profit of $112,000 isn't chicken feed."

Syl pointed to a line under operating expenses marked 'salaries.' "Especially given that it doesn't include money he put into a reserve fund to offset repairs and whatever. Plus, salaries rose substantially during the same time."

"And we can't tell whose went up?"

"No." He pointed to another line. "Utility costs also rose. A lot."

I sat down and pulled the financial statements to me. After studying them for a minute, I looked up. "I didn't hear any talk around town about the Dodsons giving employees big raises, but maybe I wouldn't. It's a private company."

"And he can certainly give himself a huge raise and little or nothing to others."

I tapped my pencil on the table. "Then why does Janet Dodson need contributions for his funeral? I don't know of any sick kids, and their house isn't in an area that floods."

"Where'd you hear she needs money?"

"Sandi told me in the diner this morning. I suppose it could be a rumor."

"You can only tell so much from financial statements, but these numbers would lead me to believe he should have some money socked away." Syl shrugged. "It's a private company. I'm surprised he let his advisory board take these statements out of the building."

I walked around the table and sifted through the stack of meeting minutes. In light pencil, Dad had placed several small exclamation points in the margin. For the last two years, he had emphasized the rise in utility costs. Another mark was next to a discussion of capital repairs. In the margin he had written "one down."

I looked up to see Syl studying me. "I can't tell you how weird it is to see my dad's notes and not be able to talk to him about them."

He nodded his always perfectly barbered head. "I get that. Do the minutes tell you more than the financial statements?"

I shrugged. "At one meeting, the operations manager mentioned that they used one less silo the last year Dad has notes for. Utility bills should have gone down. My guess is that's why he checked the utility increase discussion and the silo numbers."

"So why would they go down that much? Not like those things are heated."

I smiled. "An operating silo would use a lot of electricity to dry its grain. Otherwise, it would go bad fast. So," I flipped through a few pages of an annual report, "he has…nine of them. One down wouldn't bring utilities down one-ninth, because they have their office. But I'd expect it to be close to that amount of cost reduction."

"What do your investigative reporter skills tell you?"

I grunted. "I'm not exactly like a Watergate reporter, but I'd say, if he had someone in accounting in cahoots with him, he might have shown higher utility costs and then padded his pockets with the difference between the actual cost and what he reported."

Syl walked to the dining room window and looked onto his driveway and the now dying gladiolas I'd planted to make that area more colorful. "I could see why he'd be angry at someone, if they threatened to make their suspicions public. But even if he's caught lying, it's his company and he has no partners. I suppose, if he used the financial reports to apply for a loan and if a bank learned they're inaccurate, he could get his loan pulled."

I stood and stretched. "Big differences between what he paid farmers for their grain and the much higher price he sold it for in the spring. Maybe he said he couldn't afford to pay more."

Syl faced me. "So, they could go somewhere else."

"Not that easy. You know how we all love to drive behind trucks loaded with hogs or corn?"

He snorted.

"We farmers have to think about the cost to transport a crop. Even a few more miles reduces our potential profit. Pretty thin already."

"So using Dodson is a no-brainer."

"Bernard Hopewell owns a smaller elevator a mile from town. I heard a couple years ago that he's adding storage capacity."

"Okay, I'm showing my ignorance here. Why store it? Why not ship grain or whatever as soon as it's processed?"

"It's combined and processed in the fall. An ethanol plant might need more in the winter, but someone raising animals might want more in the …Damn!" I stood and started stuffing file folders back in a box.

"What?"

"Mister Tibbs has been inside for hours."

"Ah." Syl gathered the financial reports, then paused. "Why don't I keep these overnight? You take the rest."

"Sure." My mind was on the condition of the area rug in my sparsely furnished living room. "You can probably glean more from them than I can."

CHAPTER SEVEN

MISTER TIBBS SHOT OUT of the house like a rocket, but she had not soiled the floors. I followed and stooped to pet her, after she had thoroughly watered a spot at the base of the front porch steps. "I'm so sorry girl. I won't do that again."

She readily forgave me and wagged her tale in expectation of a walk around the yard and barn.

The warmth of the late afternoon October sun led me to take off my sweater and tie its sleeves around my waist. As we walked, I turned over what I'd read in the grain elevator meeting notes. If my father were alive, would he and others who wanted the elevator to become a co-op be suspects in Tom Dodson's death?

Everyone liked my dad. As far as I knew.

Dodson had been close to sixty. Why not take the money and retire? A couple million wasn't long-term wealth, perhaps, but in Iowa it would be darn close. Plus, he and Janet would presumably have her pension from the school system and his Social Security. They might not need to touch the money from the grain elevator sale except for special activities.

Janet would likely be picking hymns for the funeral or signing papers to buy a cemetery plot, if they didn't have one. I didn't know her well. I'd seen her be impatient in the check-out line in the grocery store, but no one had told me she was horrible to work with or a complainer to her neighbors, or anything like that. I felt bad for her.

We finished our walk, and Mister Tibbs accompanied me on several trips from the pickup to the house, me carrying a file box each time. Besides the two with farm business, a third had years of tax filings and appliance or equipment warranties. I had not taped them, but figured Mrs. Keyser had not hustled up to the attic to look in them. Or so I hoped.

When I opened the fourth box, I burst into tears. It contained several small photo albums and a bunch of loose pictures. Someone, probably Mrs. Donovan, had placed them in clear food storage bags. I almost threw the lid back onto the box.

My tears startled Mister Tibbs so much that she ran circles around me. She only stopped when I scooped her up and buried my head into her back. After a few moments, she grew antsy, so I pulled my face from her fur. I put her down when she licked my face from lips to forehead.

I told myself that the photos bothered me so much because I'd just moved back into the farmhouse. After I thoroughly washed my face, I grabbed a beer and sat on my camp chair in the living room. I spoke to Mister Tibbs as she lay in her indoor doggie bed, struggling to keep her eyes open.

"It doesn't really matter what Dad thought about the grain elevator or whether Tom Dodson was doing funny money stuff." I swallowed. "I guess he could have continued overcharging or hiding money – that's called embezzling by the way – but Ambrose and I didn't have any crops milled there the last two seasons."

Mister Tibbs yawned.

"I'm going to stack these boxes at the side of the living room, until I get shelves put up in the basement. They can stay down there until they mildew. Except the pictures."

Rumbles of thunder reached me. I had my back to the window. The sky had darkened precipitously as Mister Tibbs and I relaxed. I turned on the weather radio.

"Strong winds and quarter-size hail expected to reach South County by six p.m…."

Five-forty-five. I stood and pulled my keys out of my pocket. "You want to come with me while I park the truck in the barn?"

She did not. Mister Tibbs hates thunder.

I parked my aging pick-up in the center of the already-dark barn and dashed across the yard, making it to the house just before the purple clouds unleashed rain to douse the landscape. When I stomped on the entry rug just inside the living room door, Mister Tibbs whimpered.

"You're fine. We could use the rain. October storms usually move pretty quickly." As I said this, the intense downpour became a trickle. "Fickle weather."

Carrying the heavy boxes had made my back ache. I rarely take any medicine, but Tylenol seemed in order. I downed some, took a second beer from the fridge, so I didn't have to walk back to the kitchen in a few minutes, and sat on the side porch.

I'd grown used to living in town and being able to head to the grocery store or Mason's Diner on a whim. I loved the quiet of the farm, especially at dusk, but I missed being around people. Who would have thought I'd miss town traffic?

The combination of fitful sleep Saturday night and the beer soon had me wanting to join Mister Tibbs in la-la land. I stood, stretched, and looked down at Mister Tibbs. "Tomorrow we're going to see Bruce Blackner and then go door-to-door to leave flyers about our business. If we go to bed now, we can get up early."

She rolled over and stuck her feet in the air.

EITHER THE CRACKLE OR Mister Tibbs woke me to the orange light that flickered into my bedroom from the backyard. For a few seconds I didn't recognize the source. Then it came to me.

I jumped out of bed, stepped into a pair of sneakers without tying them, and ran onto the back porch. Had lightning struck the unusually dry cornstalks? Surely, the rain would have made them too wet to burn.

I screamed "fire!" as the orange and yellow flames moved from the burn barrel to the pile of brush I had placed next to it. Huge embers rose fifteen feet or so and drifted toward the house.

The small fire extinguisher in the kitchen would be no match, and I hadn't yet bought a new garden hose. I ran to the kitchen phone. As I dialed 9-1-1, car tires squealed in the yard.

Surely help was coming! But no, the car seemed to be speeding away from the house.

"Fire at 456 County Road 270. Perkins Place. Back yard. Hurry!"

"Are you in the house?"

"Yes, but it's just behind, moving toward the house. I'm in no danger. I'm going outside with a bucket."

Mister Tibbs' barks became more insistent.

"Stay away from the flames…"

I threw the phone onto the kitchen counter and reached below it to grab the scrub bucket from under the sink.

Had someone started a fire in my burn barrel? And what in there would burn so brightly?

The plumber had tested the outside spigot, when he turned the well pump back on. I ran outside and filled the bucket halfway before running with it toward the flames. I threw the water at the base of the burn barrel before realizing I should have thrown it on the brush pile, which was closer to the house.

Why didn't I bring out two buckets? I could have been letting one fill while I ran toward the fire with the other one.

Behind me, Mister Tibbs had grown hoarse from incessant barking. In the distance came sirens.

I heard a car slide into the front yard, and a man yelled, "Melanie!"

"I'm back here! The fire's in the back!"

Mr. Donovan ran around the corner of the house, carrying two buckets. "Let me near that spigot, girl!"

He's about seventy-five, and I'd never seen him run. When his first bucket was full, I grabbed it and shoved my empty one at him.

We got several bucketsful on the burning brush, and they began to make a dint in the flames. I couldn't imagine what was burning in the barrel.

The River's Edge Fire Department water truck pulled into the yard and barreled over two small bushes at the street side of the house to get closer to the source of the flames.

In less than one minute, stinky smoke replaced the bright orange heat. I leaned against the house, far from the burn barrel.

"Melanie!"

The anger in Mr. Donovan's voice surprised me.

"You could have slept through that fire, and it could have gotten to the house. You have to be sure you put out your barrel!"

More calmly than I felt, I said, "I didn't start that fire. I haven't used the burn barrel since I came back."

A rough man's voice asked, "What the hell do you mean?"

I recognized Gary Bradley, owner of the local tavern, Beer Rental Heaven. Apparently, he was also part of the town's volunteer firefighting squad. "What I said. I put a small bag in there Saturday morning, but didn't light it."

Gary pulled off his yellow-cornered hat. "You saying someone set that fire?"

I shrugged. "Lightning?"

"That was hours ago. And you had at least some rain out here. We didn't in town."

Another firefighter came toward us. He held the mostly charred remains of one of the white storage boxes that had held Dad's files.

"That box! They were near the street side door." I half ran up the porch step and stopped at the door that separated the kitchen from the dining room. From there I could see into the hallway. The four boxes had vanished.

Gary came up behind me. "What was in that white box?"

I swallowed, wishing I had water. "Paperwork. Mom and Dad's. I picked it up at Mrs. Keyser's this afternoon."

Mrs. Donavan's voice spoke from the kitchen. "You mean those boxes I packed for you years ago?"

I turned toward her. I'd never seen her with her hair in curlers. I managed a smile. "Yes. From Dad's file cabinet."

Mrs. Donovan looked at Gary. "I helped Melanie a bit after…well, you know. She called today to see if I remembered where she took them."

Gary looked at me. "You didn't remember?"

I frowned. "I barely remember anything from the first couple months."

He nodded. "Sure. Uh, valuable papers?"

I wasn't about to mention the Dodson Elevator files. I shook my head. "Farm business, lots of years of taxes, warranties. I think some records from committees Dad served on. Like from church. I had barely looked at them."

Mrs. Donovan's glance had gone to the firefighter's and my muddy, sooty feet. "Perhaps you should stand on the porch. I'll mop up in here."

"No, I'll do it in a minute." I gestured that we should all move toward the porch on the cornfield side of the house. "I can't thank you enough. Where's Mr. Donovan?"

"Sitting on the steps. He's tuckered."

As we began to walk out, Gary asked, "You got any writing paper, Melanie? I came from home. One of the other guys'll bring the folder with our report forms."

"Sure." I reached into a narrow kitchen drawer where I'd put stuff that had no other logical place at the moment. "And I need to bring out some glasses and water."

In five minutes, the back yard appeared bathed in sun from a huge battery-operated light on a tall pole, and several more cars were in the yard. I had no table on the porch, so Mrs. Donovan had helped herself to the TV tray by my bed. I placed on it a stack of mismatched cups, the iced tea, and a pitcher of water.

My four camp chairs were now all on the porch, and Mr. Donovan sat in one.

"Really," I began, "you two should go home. I hope all the fuss didn't wake your chickens."

"You should come sleep at our house," Mr. Donovan said.

I shook my head firmly. "The house stinks a bit from smoke blowing in, but that'll be gone soon."

Gary spoke from the bottom of the porch steps. "Maybe you should think about who got in your house to burn those boxes. When you were home, no less. With your dog."

I sat down. "I've been thinking about that. Because we were supposed to get hail, I put the truck in the barn. It could have looked like I wasn't home, but I just replaced the outside locks. No one else had a key."

Gary stared at me. "One of the panes in the door that leads to the basement, on the other side of the house, it's broken. Someone reached in."

I pictured the basement entry, through which the fire-setter had entered the house. The flight of steps was short, because the exterior door opened onto a landing. Interior steps led to either the basement or first floor.

Stooper's voice floated up the steps. "Oh, that's great. Who did you piss off, Mel?"

Gary sniggered and raised a hand to Stooper, who used to spend a lot of time in the tavern.

"Nobody!" I stared at him, flannel shirt hardly buttoned. "Who called you?"

Sheriff Gallagher spoke from behind me. "I did. Figured one of your friends might know what's going on, and Stooper was the most likely one up at four a.m."

The sheriff must have come in the front door and walked through the kitchen to the porch. He had donned his uniform in haste, as demonstrated by an untucked shirt.

I grimaced. "Thanks. I think. Why do people act as if this was my fault? I was sleeping."

The sheriff looked at Gary. "What do you need from me?"

He shrugged. "I'd say check for tire tracks, but there's maybe ten cars out there now, and they've all sloshed in the mud from the hoses. "We'll take some pictures for the county fire marshal to look at tomorrow and come back for more when it's light."

"No damage to the house?" Gallagher asked.

Gary shook his head. "Just some broken window glass. I'm gonna check all the circuit breakers in Mel's box. Doesn't look like the fire touched anything electric." He looked at me. "Couple shingles mighta got singed from an ember. We hosed the roof at the back of the house."

I rubbed both temples. "Thanks."

"Fire start in the cornfield?" Gallagher asked.

Gary gestured that Gallagher should follow him outside. "Come on out. I'll show you."

With the two men gone, the porch seemed quiet. I looked at Mr. and Mrs. Donovan. "I can never thank you enough."

He shrugged. "Didn't put out too much."

I smiled. "But hearing your voice meant help was here."

He chuckled. "I'm goin' back to bed. You don't need me."

"Melanie..." Mrs. Donovan began.

"I'll stop by tomorrow." I looked at my filthy shoes. "After I clean up."

As they left the porch, Stooper leaned down to pet Mister Tibbs, who yawned widely and leaned against him. "Didn't have time to grab you a treat." He looked up at me. "Dog wake you?"

"Eventually, but not until the fire was bright enough to light up the back yard. I don't understand why she didn't bark at whoever came in."

"Huh. Show me where they came in." When Mister Tibbs didn't seem to want to leave him alone, he bent down and picked her up. "We need to get you some remedial guard dog training."

CHAPTER EIGHT

MY HOUSE WAS EMPTY by five-thirty Monday morning. I spent a couple hours cleaning mud and soot from the porch and house floors. Then I tackled anything I could dust and put any fabric item that wasn't in a closed closet in the washer.

When I got to Mason's Diner to meet Sandi and Stooper at nine, I felt as if it were mid-afternoon. Sandi sat across from me in the booth, with Stooper next to her.

"Syl will be here in a few minutes," Stooper said. "He might be ticked you didn't call him."

Sandi glared and pulled her ponytail out of its scrunchie and then refastened it. "There's a lot of that going around."

Stooper grinned briefly. "It was Gallagher called me, not Mel."

Shirley placed my half bagel and coffee with sugar in front of me. "Shug, you need a place to stay for a bit?"

"That's really nice, Shirley, but my house doesn't even have water damage. Everything was outside."

Shirley moved away, and Sandi kind of hissed, "Except the person who broke in to get those files. That you didn't even *call* me about."

"I told you, I just picked them up at Mrs. Keyser's. Oh, she wants to find someone to rent her upstairs apartment." When Sandi glared at me some more, I added, "And I hadn't seen you."

"Syl seen 'em," Stooper said.

Sandi narrowed her eyes at me.

I shrugged. "He had a big table."

"That doesn't...," she began.

"It gave her room to spread out the paperwork." Syl slid in next to me and nodded across the room to Shirley.

Sandi and Stooper spoke together. "What paperwork?"

I shrugged. "All kinds of stuff from my dad's old file cabinet. Plus some pictures. The person only got about half of those burned before Mister Tibbs woke me up. I suppose I should be thankful for that."

"What kinds of stuff?" Sandi asked.

I took a sip of coffee. "Lots of my parents' tax records, warranty for the combine, if you must know, and, uh," I lowered my voice, "files with information from when my dad was on Tom Dodson's advisory board."

Sandi shrieked. She always does when she gets a big surprise. "What?"

Syl laughed.

Stooper and I said, "Shut up!"

Though it wasn't a busy Monday morning, the entire diner had quieted. As I looked around, conversations began again.

Shirley called, "I'll be right there, Shug."

Syl grinned. "I love this town. She wants to be in on it."

"She can have it," I murmured.

Syl pulled a newspaper clipping from the breast pocket of his blue oxford shirt. "How come the paper didn't play up your finding Mr. Dodson's body at the dinner?"

I mentally reminded myself to get the paper delivered to the farm again. I reached for the article. "I haven't seen it."

The headline blared, "**Murder at Farm Bureau Dinner.**"

For all its promise of a juicy article, the story stuck to the facts. One paragraph was based on an interview with the Farm Bureau president, who pointed out that someone not in attendance could have come in, killed Tom Dodson, and left.

The article ended with a quote from Sheriff Gallagher. "At this point, we have no suspect or motive. Sometime Monday, we should have more information about Mr. Dodson's cause of death."

I handed it back to Syl and raised my eyebrows toward Sandi. "Balanced. Did you write that?"

She shook her head. "Ryan. Scott told him he couldn't mention you, because too little was known. He didn't want to make it seem as if you were a suspect."

Stooper finished a glass of orange juice. "Mighty good of him."

Syl didn't hide a smile. "They could get around to it later."

"Thanks a lot." I frowned at Sandi. "I thought you would write it."

She shook her head. "I interview. Ryan writes on topics related to you."

My chirping cell phone kept me from commenting. I glanced at the screen. "Bruce Blackner. I have to see him today."

"Insurance?" Syl asked.

"Kind of." I didn't say that Bruce had previously told me to stop by today. It was too weird. "Hello, Bruce."

I listened as he expressed relief that I was okay and repeated that I should come by.

"How about in maybe an hour? I need to stop by the sheriff's for a few minutes."

I hung up, as Stooper asked, "Does Gallagher investigate when it's a fire?"

I shrugged. "I think he looks for the person who started it, and the fire guys try to figure out technically how it started. Except in this case, who cares if it was a lighter or a match?"

"Who knew you had those boxes?" Sandi asked.

I frowned. "It probably depends on how many people Mrs. Keyser talked to yesterday."

"At least, you know you're onto something," Syl said.

"I wasn't looking for anything."

Sandi tapped her oatmeal spoon on the table. "What kind of grain elevator records? Are they all gone?"

Thankfully, Syl said nothing.

"I looked at some yesterday. Meeting agendas, notes, couple annual reports. No death threats issued three years ago."

"Very funny," Sandi said.

"What kind of death threats?" Stooper asked.

I sighed. "I meant the files said nothing about whether Dodson had people in his life who wanted him dead. That kind of thing."

Stooper shrugged. "Lots of farmers wanted a co-op, because they thought they'd run the elevator better and could maybe charge less."

"Here's the thing," Syl said. "Why do you call a bunch of farm silos an elevator? And if that's the right word, why not elevators?"

I smiled. "The individual silos are just that. You know when you see what looks like several sort of together, with a taller part at one end?"

"Kind of," Syl said.

"The elevator is the tower, the tall part, often square. It has a bucket elevator, maybe a pneumatic conveyor. It scoops up grain from a lower level and puts it in a silo. Or a truck or some other storage facility or transport vehicle."

Seeing Syl's expression, Stooper added, "The whole operation is just called the elevator. You'd have a helluva a hard time moving grain without the hydraulics."

"So, if I have one of those conical things, I just have a silo?" Syl asked.

We all nodded.

Shirley's shadow graced our booth's table, and she plopped coffee in front of Syl. "Now that you all are through with the farm lesson, will someone please tell me what in God's name is going on?"

I put my palms up in an exaggerated shrug. "All I can tell you is I woke up and my burn barrel was on fire big time, with a bunch of files I'd just gotten out of storage. You know, because I'm bringing things back to the house."

Shirley leaned over. "You left out the dead body at the Farm Bureau basket dinner."

I tried to appear conspiratorial. "But I expect you to tell us all about that. I mean, you've been here, what, two... Hey, weren't you getting a perm today?"

Shirley flushed. "Didn't work out."

"You just came in..." I began.

She turned. "I got toast on in the kitchen."

"Toast my ass," Sandi said.

"Maybe the paper should hire her," Syl suggested.

Stooper left for Dr. Carver's house to finish raking leaves, and Sandi wanted to find the Farm Bureau president, who I expected was in hiding somewhere.

Syl was about to leave for Des Moines. When we were alone, he said, "I scanned those financial reports last night. Have the originals in my desk and copies on my laptop. You want me to email them?"

I counted out change for a tip. "If people can break into my house, maybe they can hack."

He shrugged. "I didn't know if you'd want them now. I'll be back tomorrow night. Is that soon enough to get them to you? I guess I could swing back home."

I shook my head. "I kind of like not having them. For now."

As I stood, he asked, "Why didn't you tell Sandi about them?"

"I trust her, but not the people she works with. There's nothing to connect my father or me with Dodson's death. But somebody at the paper would mention I found his body and that my dad's old files had those financial reports from the elevator." I scowled. "And they'll make it sound like any disagreements between the two of them were a big deal."

"Even though it was all a long time ago?"

"Even though."

MY NEXT STOP WAS THE law enforcement building. The jail is part of the same structure, and the courthouse is next door. You can get booked and tried within a block.

Sheriff Gallagher's receptionist and do-anything-except-wear-a-badge, Sophie pointed a finger at me as I entered the sheriff's building.

"The sheriff asked me to stop by this morning. Is he in?"

Sophie nodded. "He said to let him know as soon as you came by."

That struck me as odd. Because the burn barrel fire was set and could have taken out my house, it was certainly a crime. But with Dodson's murder, I figured the sheriff had a lot more to do than make me a priority.

Sophie used her phone to buzz the sheriff, and looked at me as she hung up. "I'll push a button here, and the door to the offices will unlock."

I thanked her and entered the hallway that led to several offices, a small conference room and, at the far end, a door to the sally port where deputies brought in people they arrested. Sheriff Gallagher's was the largest office, room for a table even, and I thought was the third one on the left. I went to it and knocked on the door jamb.

Without looking up from something he was writing, he said, "Come on in, Melanie."

I sat across from him and took in the blonde wood furniture, which was like a lot of teachers' desks, and the framed items on the wall behind him. He still belonged to the Iowa Sheriff's and Deputies Association, but now also had a letter of thanks from the governor for leadership on a regional drug task force.

After maybe twenty or thirty seconds, he put his pen down. "Thanks for stopping by. I need to know what was in those files that was so special. Or someone considered a threat."

"A threat?"

"Whoever wanted those files burned poured fire-starter in the barrel. So yeah, I'm thinking they didn't want anyone seeing what was in them."

"Good question. Don't know much. I picked them up at Mrs. Keyser's yesterday." I repeated Mrs. Donovan's role in initially packing them and her help in prodding my memory, as to where I took them. "I hadn't given them a thought since I carted them to that attic more than two years ago."

"What made you think to get them now?"

"They were my dad's files. Luckily, Ken Brownberg still has the deed. He needed it to respond to Frost's lawsuit. I wouldn't have thought of them, if a couple people hadn't mentioned Dad had words with Tom Dodson and…"

Gallagher had been jotting notes on a small spiral-bound pad, but stopped. "Who said that?"

"I told you Saturday night that after I registered for the Farm Bureau dinner Tom called me. From others, I heard any disagreement had to do with GMO seed and maybe costs. You know, at the elevator."

"Others?"

"Let's see. I asked Ambrose, but he didn't know much. Andy at the hardware store acted like he did, but he ticked me off, so I left."

Gallagher scowled and jotted down Andy's name. "So, all those files dealt with some sort of dispute at the elevator? Was this a legal matter? I don't remember it."

I shook my head. "Lots of business stuff related to our farm, personal files like utility bills."

"Nothing to do with Dodson or the elevator?"

You'd be stupid to lie to the sheriff. "Dad was on his advisory board for a couple of years. He had files of minutes, annual reports."

"Aren't those public documents?"

"It's not a public entity, not even like a co-op that would share some business data with its members."

He leaned back in his extra-wide office chair. "Lots of controversy?"

I narrowed my eyes as I looked at him, but just enough to convey that I was skeptical about this question. "My guess is you've heard all this."

"Some. Certainly not that your father had those files. Jeb Nelson called this morning. He thought it strange that someone was trying to burn boxes at your place right after Dodson was killed. He gave me some background."

"Oh, good. Does he still have his copies of the minutes? Once Janet Dodson started doing them, they got pretty sparse."

Gallagher shook his head. "Not long after your parents died, Dodson announced he was changing the meetings from advising him to simple briefings to elevator customers. He invited more people, and Jeb said they were really just an opportunity for him to say how great they were."

"So, Dad might have even been at the last actual advisory board meeting?" I didn't know that it mattered, but the fact that the meetings had been discontinued after his death bothered me. I wasn't sure why.

Gallagher pointed his pencil at me. "And Dodson asked all committee members to turn in their copies of minutes and financial reports. Except, of course, your dad's."

I stared at him, unseeing for a moment.

"You okay?" Gallagher asked.

"Yes, just thinking how coincidental that Dad's files may have been the last detailed info about elevator operations that outsiders had seen."

"And the contents of all the boxes were burned?"

I nodded slowly. That was the honest truth. Anything in those boxes had burned. "Luckily the fourth box was family photos, and I heard they didn't all make it into the barrel. You have them, I think."

"I'm having those checked for prints, then I'll give them back. The covers seem to have protected the contents from the fire hoses.

The guys have tried to pull latent prints from a couple of them, and they're faded and smudged. I'd say from before your parents died, so probably not useful."

"That's fast work. You almost make me think that you see some relationship between Tom's murder and my dad's files."

"I don't believe in coincidences. You telling me everything?"

I did a palms up shrug. "I had no idea he was on the advisory group. Or that he and Dodson disagreed on stuff." I paused. "My dad had a reputation for getting along with everyone."

"Sorry to say I didn't know him and your mother well, but that's the kind of thing I've heard about them."

"Are you allowed to tell me anything about Tom Dodson's murder?"

Gallagher frowned. "No, except to say I have no idea who did it or why. Stay out of it."

"Do you even know how he died?"

Gallagher frowned. "No details, and not your business." He flipped to the back of his legal pad, glanced at a list of questions, then went back to the front page on which he'd been taking notes.

I smiled. "You had to write down questions to grill me on?"

He grunted. "Didn't get a lot of sleep. Two more things."

"Yes?"

"Who knew you had those boxes? Or would have cared?"

"I had just picked them up from Mrs. Keyser that day."

"So, she knew. Who else?"

"Just Syl. I stopped at his place, and he volunteered his dining room table to spread out the files."

Gallagher stared at me some more.

"I guess I don't know who else Mrs. Keyser told I stopped by to get the boxes, but she had no idea what was in them."

He grunted. "Were they taped shut?"

"No."

"Knowing her, she looked through them when you first put them up there. I'll see who she talked to."

I shrugged. "If she remembered I had files related to Dodson, it might have been good fodder for the beauty shop, but it wasn't open on Sunday. She wouldn't have had time to tell anyone."

Some thought dinged in my brain, but it escaped.

"Final question. For now. How in the hell did you not hear someone enter your house and remove those files?"

"Not just me, but Mister Tibbs."

"Dog didn't wake you up?"

"Eventually she barked. I think about the same time the light from the fire came into my bedroom. The burn barrel wasn't directly outside my room, and I'd had a couple of beers and Tylenol before I went to sleep."

"Me, I'da heard someone in my living room. Or my dog would've."

I shrugged. "They came in from a side door that leads to the basement, nowhere near my bedroom. Without the beer and the…let's say emotional turmoil of the weekend, I wouldn't have been sleeping so soundly."

He put his pen down. "If those boxes were full of paper, they were heavy. The person who burned them probably made at least two or three trips from the house to the burn barrel. You think your dog could have known the person? Been willing to let them wander in and out?"

"She's friendly. She might have yipped at first, but if someone expected to see her, they may have had a biscuit. She's kind of a whore for treats."

"You're lucky you weren't killed."

CHAPTER NINE

VERY LUCKY. I DOUBTED the fire would have gotten close enough to kill me, but if I'd had my bedroom window open, the smoke could have. Though I figured Mister Tibbs would have barked enough to get me up, I still felt queasy every time I thought of the fire.

I didn't understand why she hadn't alerted me to someone being in the house. That would imply she knew the person, but no one I knew would break into my house.

As I unlocked my truck in the law enforcement parking lot, I thought about Sheriff Gallagher's questions about Mister Tibbs. Had whoever entered given her a treat laced with some sort of sleep medicine? Obviously, she didn't fall asleep, or at least stay asleep.

Was I willing to take her for a blood draw at the vet's? Mostly, I didn't want to subject myself to taking her there. Still, she'd seemed extra tired today, but so was I.

I glanced at my watch. Mister Tibbs had been alone less than two hours. I'd told Bruce Blackner an hour. I needed to go help Stooper at Dr. Carver's place, but once I started digging in the soil I'd be too dirty for a meeting in town. I would do what I needed to in town and see if I could get an appointment for Mister Tibbs with our vet, Joshua Marshall.

I called the veterinary clinic and told the receptionist, Annette, that I was concerned Mister Tibbs might have been given some sort of drug.

"My goodness, Melanie, do you think you should bring her right over?"

I remembered how much she liked her. "I have a couple things to do first. I think she's okay, I mostly want to know if Mister Tibbs ingested or was given some kind of sedative last night."

Annette scheduled a time for Mister Tibbs to get a blood test. "But Dr. Marshall won't know anything until tomorrow."

"That's fine. I'm probably being silly."

Usually I walked around downtown, but today I wasn't in the mood to chat with whomever I might run into on the street. I felt as if my return to life at the farm had been spoiled.

Like nearly every business in town, Bruce Blackner's insurance agency sat at street level. I parked in front of his burgundy awning.

The entry bell jingled as I opened the door. He rarely has anyone at the receptionist's desk, so I called out. "Bruce? Melanie here."

His voice came down the hall. "Come on back." He continued talking, and I realized he was on the phone. But he'd said come back, so I did.

As I walked in, he hung up and gestured at the captain's chair opposite his huge, burnished cherry desk. "Good to see you. Sorry to hear about the fire last night."

"No damage to the house, except maybe a couple singed shingles."

Bruce tented his fingers and glanced at some papers on his desk.

I didn't understand why he seemed uncomfortable. "What did you want to talk to me about?"

"Kind of a moot point now. If I'd known you were going to the dinner, I'd have talked to you last week."

"About Dad and Tom Dodson?"

"More the opinion of your dad and some others about the elevator. Didn't want someone to bring it up and you be put in the position of asking questions."

"I only know he and Jeb Nelson and maybe a couple others thought it would be good if Dodson sold it to a group to make it a co-op." I ignored the GMO issue.

He nodded. "They thought it could be operated with fewer expenses, and of course, there's no CEO to pay a high salary to."

"I don't think co-op managers work for free."

He shook his head. "The people managing operations are usually salaried. Co-op board members might get an honorarium-type payment, not a salary."

"And the finances are public?" Maybe I could find published ones online and compare costs to those at Dodson Grain Elevator.

"Among the co-op members," Blackner said.

"But it was Tom's decision. Why would people feel a need to bring it up to me now?"

"Your father pushed hardest for Tom selling so a co-op could be formed. After your dad's death, a couple folks wanted to hire a lawyer to make an offer, but that didn't go anywhere."

I glanced around his formally decorated office, with its dark paneling and thick carpet. Nothing indicated most of his clients were rural businesses. "If you don't mind me asking, how do you know so much about this?"

"Discussed with your father about how insurance would work if they created a co-op."

"Sounds as if he thought it could really happen."

"From the way he talked, I thought he and Dodson had met one-on-one about it. Your father said something about creating the right incentives." Blackner laughed. "I figured he'd give Tom some cruise brochures or something."

Or maybe he told Tom Dodson that he thought actual expenses couldn't be as high as those in the financial reports and asked where that money went.

Bruce interrupted my thoughts. "There's one more thing."

I forced a smile. "All advice welcome."

He leaned back in his chair and the leather upholstery emitted a sound between a squeak and a groan. "You know when I bought Hal's boat, I went through that so-called novel he left onboard."

"Sure. So-called is a good way to phrase it."

"You surely noticed he used circumstances strikingly similar to your parents' car accident."

I swallowed bile that rose in my throat. "Even giving his characters similar names."

"Hadn't noticed that. It was a tragic accident. I didn't want you to hear from someone else that a couple people in town wondered whether someone had fooled with their car."

I watched a stink bug crawl a couple of inches across his blotter and idly wondered how one of the fall bugs had made its way into his office. I supposed they didn't care where they went, as long as it was warmer than outside.

Blackner slid the bug into a tissue and tossed it into his trash can. "Melanie?"

I started. "Sorry. I never heard anyone say anything about someone fooling with…tampering with my parents' car. No one we know would do that."

He pointed a finger at me. "Exactly. Your parents were well liked. No one would have any reason to harm them."

Except maybe an embezzler who worked at the grain elevator. I wondered if Tom Dodson should have been a suspect in their deaths and if he was devious enough to cover it up.

I HAD TOLD THE Donovans I would stop by, so I swung into their driveway before going to my place. Incessant clucking came from behind their house. With all the noise last night, I bet the chickens were off their usual schedule.

The Donovan barn was behind the house instead of across from it, so they had a front lawn with shrubs and flower beds. A couple stalwart zinnias still bloomed in one of the three beds, but the other annuals had been cleared for winter.

Mr. Donovan opened the door and gestured that I should enter. "You look better than I thought you would."

I grinned. "I could say the same to you."

He went to get his wife while I admired the blue and white tile, bright yellow walls, and replica of an old washstand with a white bowl and pitcher. They won a nice sum from a scratch-off ticket not long ago and had used much of it to modernize their home.

Mrs. Donovan came into the living room and gestured that I should sit in one of the two blue upholstered chairs. She took the other. "I didn't hear you knock, dear. Goodness, you've had a time."

I sat, and Mr. Donovan sank onto the couch. He did look tired. "I'm okay. I wanted to thank you again for last night."

He waved a hand. "You would've done the same. Has the sheriff caught anyone?"

"No. I just stopped by there. He thinks it's really strange that someone wanted to burn those files. I agree."

Mrs. Donovan said, "We do, too. We heard at the senior center this morning that your dad had kept some of the Dodson Elevator files. With Tom's death, we wondered if that's why someone wanted them destroyed. But in your burn barrel? Land's sake."

Great. Mrs. Keyser's been blabbing. "I just remembered Tom was in line to be Farm Bureau president next year. Does that mean you'll be staying on as secretary?"

Mrs. Donovan almost huffed. "I found out at the dinner that Brenda Chase was who he was going to ask to do it. She came up and said he told her I would help her with the...what did she say?" She looked at her husband.

He grinned. "Grunt stuff. Obviously, Tom Dodson didn't know my wife well."

Mrs. Donovan pursed her lips for a second. "There's a very small stipend that comes with doing the minutes and everything else the secretary does. I think Tom asked her to do it and told her she'd get paid and I'd still do most of the work."

Mr. Donovan shrugged. "She was probably one of his bed buddies."

I laughed aloud, and Mrs. Donovan shook a finger at him. "Now, he's passed."

"Doesn't change who he was," he said.

I WENT HOME TO GET Mister Tibbs for a trip to the vet clinic. I had trouble thinking of Tom Dodson as some kind of stud. The best word to describe his looks would have been ordinary.

I pushed aside thoughts about Tom, as I placed Mister Tibbs on the truck seat next to me. "Okay, you won't like this, but then you get to see Stooper."

Her tail thumped, and she looked out the window of the truck, as if expecting me to pull into a familiar yard and see his beat-up Dodge Dart. She was less happy when I pulled into Dr. Marshall's parking lot.

"It's okay. Just a little stick, and we'll be on our way." I kept a short leash in the truck and clipped it to her collar.

Annette let us into an examining room, and I was surprised when Dr. Marshall himself came in with paraphernalia for a blood draw.

He ruffled the curls on Mister Tibbs' head. "What makes you think someone might have given her something?"

I recounted her lack of reaction to last night's intruder. "It wasn't until the light from flames came into my bedroom that she barked."

"Huh." He pulled one of her eyelids up and peered at her. "A bit dull, but I suppose she didn't sleep much." He reached into a drawer to pull out a treat and tossed it a few inches above her head.

Mister Tibbs leapt up, but missed the treat as it came toward her. She easily scooped it off the metal table.

"I'd have expected her to grab that in the air. Let's do a blood draw and see what comes up."

I kept Mister Tibbs' eyes focused on mine and told her she was a good girl. Dr. Marshall had the blood he needed in a matter of seconds.

"I'll call you in the morning."

He left the room, and I refastened her leash. "Now we go see Stooper."

I spent two hours working with Stooper to spread a huge amount of mulch around every bush and flowerbed in Dr. Carver's yard. Mister Tibbs tried to catch bits of mulch as we threw it on the beds.

After every attempt, she sat for a few seconds. I told myself she was simply pooped. Eventually she caught a couple pieces and realized she didn't want to chew wood.

The mindless mulching task was perfect as I considered the implications of what Bruce Blackner had told me.

Earlier this year, I wondered and discarded the idea that Peter Frost wanted my parents dead so he could get their land. I had not considered my parents' death anything other than the wintry accident it surely was. Had to be.

But what made Hal think otherwise when he was writing his book? Or was he just being his usual troublemaking self?

I pieced together events of that awful night. I lived at the farmhouse, in what my father joked was my apartment. Pay was low at the paper, and my parents and I never got on each other's nerves.

In any event, Mom had made a cheese and broccoli chicken casserole and a batch of brownies to take to their supper with friends who lived just north of Keosauqua. I mentioned to Dad that the temperature might get low enough for rain to turn to sleet, and he said he'd looked at the forecast, too, and didn't expect sleet or freezing rain until close to dawn.

I shivered. What he'd said was that he and Mom would be "sleeping soundly" by the time sleet made the roads slippery.

"Mel?"

Stooper's voice brought me back to the present, and I realized I had tears on my cheeks.

"You okay? That doesn't look like allergies or somethin'."

I wiped a gloved hand across my cheeks. "I was thinking about my parents."

I suspected Stooper's frown and glance at Dr. Carver's porch indicated panic. I smiled. "I'm okay, really. Bruce Blackner said some bozos talked about whether their car accident was somehow…planned."

His frown deepened. "As in your parents sure as hell weren't the folks who planned it?"

The combination of Stooper's uncertainty about how to handle my tears and the absurd way he described a possible murder made me laugh. And laugh. And sit on the ground with my knees drawn to my chest and face buried in my hands.

Mister Tibbs barked from the other side of the yard, and I could hear her running toward me.

Stooper sat next to me. After a few seconds, he said, "I didn't know your folks well, but I never heard anyone say one bad thing." He pulled Mr. Tibbs from where she was trying to climb onto my knees. She began to sniff him for treats.

I jerked up my head and looked at him. "Did you carve their headstone?" *How could I not know that?*

"It was one of the last ones my old man did." His smile reflected bitterness. "I did keep watch on him to be sure he didn't spell nothing wrong."

Something warm began to leak from my nose, and I sniffed mightily.

Stooper grinned. "One time in high school, Mrs. Simmons caught me wiping my nose on the back of my sleeve. She handed me a Kleenex and asked the class if they knew why the queen's guards, the guys with the big hats, had buttons on their jackets. Near the cuff."

"Did anyone know?"

He shook his head, still smiling. "Mrs. Simmons said it was 'cause some queen saw them wipe their noses on their sleeves and she didn't want them doin' that."

I took this as permission to wipe my nose, but used the back of my glove. "She never told my class that story. Sounds like one of hers."

Stooper appeared relieved to see me calmer.

He began to scramble to his feet, no simple proposition for him. "Can't believe your ass isn't cold."

"Jeez Louise. It is." Back on our feet, we faced each other. "Thanks a lot."

His nod was somber. "People don't have enough to do, they make up sh…stuff."

Without saying anything else, we got back to work. I'm not a big fan of mulch so, in a few minutes, I was ready to go to the garden center at the hardware store to get a bunch of tulip bulbs. They were a present of sorts for Dr. Carver. If she didn't want spring flowers, I could dig them up.

Stooper threw a rake and shovel in the back of my pick-up. "You gonna get some of those decorated cabbage plants for the pots downtown?"

I decided not to tell him the word was decorative. "Good idea. I was going to do it tomorrow, but why wait?"

"You get 'em, I'll help you plant the square tomorrow."

Stooper and I had persuaded a bunch of town businesses to put huge planters in front of their stores or offices. We filled them with good Iowa dirt and some topsoil and put in plants. Business owners were to water the ones in front of their shops. That kept our costs fairly low.

Most of the store or business owners had agreed to have us dig up the potted annuals and put in pansies and decorative cabbage plants. They survived in cooler weather, though usually for a few weeks at most. Nothing fragile survived an Iowa winter.

Since mulch spreading hadn't gotten me grimy, Mister Tibbs and I drove back toward town. I debated whether to stop by Mrs. Keyser's to see who she talked to after I left her yesterday. I thought she was likely to mention that I'd been interested in boxes in her attic, even though I hadn't touched them since I put them up there.

The dropping temperature meant I'd go to the square first, to try to drum up more business, then Mrs. Keyser's warm sitting room. I headed for the small variety store.

When I got to Mr. Patel's door, the black cat that had adopted him last summer wound herself through my legs. Or himself. I didn't know.

I opened the door to the store, and Mr. Patel surprised me by yelling, "Out. You know you can't come in here!"

The cat slid back out, and he grumbled, "My wife is allergic. I wish I never started feeding that damn cat." He reached under his chipped wooden counter and pulled out a bag of cat food.

I thought the cat fit the décor of scuffed wood floors and a jumble of merchandise that was a combination of street bazaar and dollar store. The modern cash register looked as if it had landed in the wrong century.

Mr. Patel fed the cat and went back to his counter, where I joined him. "What can I do for you, Melanie?"

I wanted to mention the plants, but instead asked, "Where will the cat stay in the winter?"

He ran one hand through thinning black hair. "I'll put a box behind the store. Unless…" He appeared hopeful. "You want it."

I recalled that Mister Tibbs was not fond of the animal. But I also needed what my mother called a mouser – a cat that would keep the farm rodent population under control.

"I'm not really in the market, but I don't want it to end up in a box in the alley. How about I check back in a few days? Maybe you'll have found another home for it."

With that cheery prospect, from Mr. Patel's perspective, he agreed to the twenty-five dollar charge for me to clean his pot of summer plants and add the decorative cabbage.

I petted the cat as I left. It slunk under my pick-up. Cats are smart. I knew it would get out of the way when I started the engine.

This cat was especially canny. When I opened the driver's side door, it appeared at my foot and jumped into the cab.

CHAPTER TEN

TO MAKE IT HARDER TO grab him/her/it, the cat climbed into the truck's back seat. I stayed on the pavement but glanced behind the front seat until my eyes found its yellow ones. "You decided to go for a ride?"

I glanced at Mister Tibbs. She had been lying on the back seat, behind my seat. I laughed at her expression. "He's cold. Or it is. He won't bother you."

As I shut the truck door, the cat curled its tail around itself and settled in for a snooze. Mister Tibbs' expression, to the extent dogs have them, was pleading.

I walked back into the store. Mr. Patel called from the back that he would be right with me, and I leaned against the counter. I did not want a cat, but it apparently did not want to be outside. I could take it with me and find it another home.

"What's up, Melanie?"

"Since your cat jumped into my truck, I should probably get whatever food and litter you have for it."

His brow furrowed, then he smiled. "It picked you."

"Lucky me. If Mister Tibbs is apoplectic, I'll find it a good home. Is it an it?"

He shrugged. "My brother-in-law says it's a neutered boy. It's not exactly a lap cat, so I haven't looked." He turned toward the back of his store. "Be right back."

Mr. Patel's mention of a brother-in-law reminded me that he owned stores in three small Southeast Iowa towns. He had once characterized his business as one that did not make him wealthy, but kept his brothers-in-law in jobs.

Before he returned, Mrs. Patel swished to the front of the store in a brightly colored sari. "Melanie. You are such a dear. I just hated to see that poor animal so cold in the morning."

She drew close and kissed my cheek.

You could've let him into a back room. "No problem. He may even catch a few mice on the farm."

Metallic clanging announced Mr. Patel. He had a bag of litter in one hand, and a couple metal cat food dishes in the other. One bounced to the floor.

"I'll get it." I walked a few feet to pick up the bowl. "This will all come in handy."

He passed his wife without stopping. "Take the bag of food from under the counter, and I'll put these things in Melanie's truck."

He did so, and as I was about to climb into the truck with the food, I called to him. "What's his name?"

Mr. Patel shrugged. "I just call him Cat."

I climbed in and started the engine. The cat meowed and strode onto the console that separates the front and back seats.

"Animals sit in the back."

Mister Tibbs yipped, as if to endorse this position.

Cat bounded to the floor on the front passenger side and pawed at the food bag. I put the truck back in park and reached down to unfasten the bag's clip and take out a few pieces of dry food. "You don't look like you've missed any meals."

He gulped the food and looked up, clearly expecting more.

"I can tell you're going to be a lot of trouble."

SINCE THE TEMPERATURE WAS in the upper forties, I felt comfortable leaving Cat in the car when I went into her house to talk to Mrs. Keyser. I took Mister Tibbs and tied her to a porch column. When I glanced back, the cat was on its hind legs, paws on the front passenger window.

Mrs. Keyser opened the door before I knocked. Today's house dress had a fall harvest scene, with dried corn on one side of the snaps and a basket of apples on the other. The apples were placed unfortunately high.

"Melanie. Looking for more boxes?" She stood aside so I could enter.

Clearly, she had not heard about the fire in my burn barrel. How could that be? When she coughed into a tissue, I realized she didn't feel good.

I followed her into her sitting room. "Sorry you have a cold."

"I've been drinking tea with honey all day. I had bronchitis last year. I don't want to be cooped up with that again."

I remembered her bout. I'd brought her soup a couple of times, and her daughter came down from Minnesota for the weekend. Because it had been mid-winter and Mrs. Keyser avoids ice, I hadn't thought of her as cooped up. The cold did explain her lack of burn barrel info.

She sat in her rocker, and I sat on the couch, careful to avoid her cat's placemat. "You know that black cat Mr. Patel had at his shop?"

"Lands yes. He asked me to take it."

"It hopped into my truck today. We'll see how it does on the farm."

She dabbed at her nose. "Do you need to borrow some food?"

"He gave me some. You can help me with one thing. Not a cat thing."

I began by telling her Mister Tibbs was fine, and launched into the events of last night. She sat perfectly still, hanging on every word.

"But your house is fine? You didn't hear anyone come in? Who would burn your boxes?"

All good fodder for the beauty shop. "My bedroom is nowhere near where the person broke some door glass to come in, and it's not near the side door where I had the boxes. I guess that's how they carried them out without me hearing."

"With you in the house!"

"Because the forecast called for hail, my truck was in the barn. The person may not have known I was home until I got up and yelled fire."

She frowned. "I suppose that's reassuring. Is there something I can do for you?"

"I wondered if you had any idea about who knew I brought those boxes from your attic to my house."

Her mouth opened but she said nothing. Her eyes darted around the living room.

"I'm not mad if you happened to mention it to anyone. Just…curious."

"I went down to Hy-Vee for cat food. Let's see. I, well. I talked to one of the high school teachers in the check-out line. And Eliza Wright was buying canned pumpkin for her pies." She paused.

Great. The one person who blabs more than you do. I forced a smile. "My mom grew pie pumpkins, but I use the canned pumpkin, too. Anyone else?"

"Some other people were in the pie aisle, but I didn't know them. So many new people in town these days."

I didn't agree with the 'many,' but from her perspective as a seventy-plus year resident, it likely seemed that way.

"On the way home, I saw the lights on in the beauty shop." She leaned forward. "You know it's usually closed Sunday and Monday."

I nodded. Someone else had mentioned the beauty shop. Who was that?

"So, of course, I got out to check. Sylvia was doing Janet Dodson's hair. Wasn't that nice?"

Right, Janet. As my stomach clenched, we spent close to a minute talking about Sylvia's good nature and her occasional task to style someone, a former someone, at the funeral home. Mrs. Keyser had, of course, been let in to give Janet a hug.

Finally, I asked, "Did you happen to mention the boxes?"

"Well, I'd just seen you."

I almost laughed. She had, from her perspective, hot news, and the beauty parlor was open on an off day. She must have thought she'd won the lottery.

Except it wasn't funny.

I didn't want to ask her point blank if she'd talked about the boxes' content. "Now that we have the farm back, I was really glad to get all of Dad's business records."

"And I bet you were pleased as punch to find the box of photos, too." Perhaps realizing that she'd just confessed to going through my stuff, she blanched.

I pretended her busybody nature didn't bother me and smiled. "I had a few others, so it was mostly the records I wanted."

She nodded several times.

Yep, she told Janet Dodson that my boxes had info on the grain elevator.

BY THE TIME I got home, Mister Tibbs was again anxious to do her business. I left the cat in the truck, planning to bring her into the house when Mister Tibbs was settled after her sprint around the yard.

Cat stood on his hind legs, at the window. Mister Tibbs emitted a low growl.

"Nuts." I stooped to pet Mister Tibbs. "Wouldn't you like some company?"

Another growl said otherwise.

"Look, it's likely temporary. I'll put him in the spare bedroom tonight. With the door shut."

Mister Tibbs turned and ran up the steps onto the porch. I let her in, took a dog treat from its jar, and carried it to my bedroom. She followed, and as she ate, I shut the door. "Just for a few minutes."

I couldn't believe I had important issues to deal with and I'd have to spend a good part of the evening playing referee between two animals. I put saucers of milk and water on the floor in the kitchen.

When I got back to the pickup, Cat stood in greeting. I spoke through the window. "I'll carry the litter and food, and you can follow me into the house." I had debated carrying him, but he'd doubtless have none of it. Plus, cat bites usually get infected.

I opened the truck door. He bounded out and sniffed Mister Tibbs' trail to the porch. I had the food, so I wasn't worried that he'd wander. When I opened the door to the house, he marched in as if he'd lived there for years.

His metal cat bowl had food when he found me in the kitchen, having completed a first tour of the house. Since I have little furniture, it hadn't taken him long to check the two open bedrooms and bath. I had kept my bedroom door closed.

His spot would be a towel on one of my two dining room chairs. He thought otherwise and hopped in my recliner. He let me lift him from there onto the towel. "That's your spot. Don't beat up Mister Tibbs."

When I approached my closed bedroom door, Mister Tibbs whimpered. She was on my bed when I entered. "You don't get up there." She walked in circles several times but did not lie down.

I picked her up. "I know this is scary, but you're tough. Pretend we have a weekend guest."

When we got to the living room, Cat looked up from his chair but did not get up. *So far so good.* I sat Mister Tibbs on the floor a couple feet from the chair.

She approached slowly. Cat was on his side and leaned just his large head over the edge of the chair. They sniffed from a distance of about twelve inches. No hisses or growls.

Mister Tibbs turned and moved closer to me. Her eyes said traitor, so I picked her up again. "It'll be okay." I put her down, and she wandered back to my bedroom. She keeps her chew toys in her bed. I would have to get a couple of cat toys. No catnip.

"Whew."

Cat eyed me as I pulled my phone from a pocket, then he curled into a ball.

Who should I let know that Mrs. Keyser had blabbed about the contents of my boxes? The sheriff, eventually. He had told me to stay out of his murder investigation, but hadn't said I shouldn't talk to people about the burn barrel.

Before I called the sheriff to say Mrs. Keyser had broadcast my file boxes' contents, I wanted to talk to a friend. Usually that would be Sandi, but she'd been assigned the story. Or maybe just the Dodson murder, maybe not the theft and burning of what had most recently been my files.

No, she'd have both. Scott Holmes knew I wouldn't deal with Ryan, and he didn't want to bother with me.

That left Syl or Stooper. I opted for Syl and punched in his number on my phone. "I might have figured out some of the people who knew I brought the boxes home."

"That was fast."

"I have someone new for you to meet. Can you come over?"

Syl said nothing for a few seconds. "It's not that high school principal from the Farm Bureau dinner, is it? Jeez, the person isn't there, are they?"

I laughed. "I wouldn't do that to you. You go to Mr. Patel's store?"

"God, he suckered you into taking the black cat."

"Cat's choice. I have stuff for spaghetti."

"Okay. I just got home. Half an hour?"

"Dinner will be ready in an hour, but you can come anytime."

For a change, he didn't ask if he should bring Stooper.

CHAPTER ELEVEN

MY DINING ROOM HELD only four mismatched chairs and the small thrift-shop table that used to sit in my apartment's kitchen. We had room for Syl, me, our spaghetti, and the sheets of paper he'd brought and placed at one end of the table.

I laid out my thoughts about why Janet Dodson was a good candidate for the burn barrel firebug. Mostly because she knew about the files. I had no idea what she thought was in them.

Syl sliced some garlic bread. "She could know the significance of the files, but my guess would be your Mrs. Keyser didn't get into the contents of individual folders."

"Probably not. But Sheriff Gallagher said Jeb Nelson told him Tom Dodson collected all the reports and such from other committee members. If she knew about hanky-panky with the financial statements, she'd want them."

"Why? He's gone, and she didn't do it."

"As far as we know." I drank some iced tea. "Did I tell you that, when she knelt next to Tom, she said, 'It was just getting better'?"

Syl stopped with bread halfway to his mouth, and his eyebrows went up. "No, and I don't think you mentioned it to Sheriff Gallagher that night."

"I didn't, but several people heard it. I suppose I should bring it up, in case no one else thought to tell him."

Syl chewed his bite of bread for several seconds. "Kind of funny, though. Her husband just died. Wouldn't a bunch of people be with her? Someone would know that she snuck out at two or three in the morning."

I pointed my fork at him. "And she would have smelled of smoke when she got home. Although…" I closed my eyes for two seconds. "When she called me to apologize for accusing me of killing her husband, she said her daughter was arriving this morning."

Syl nodded slowly. "So, she could have been alone last night."

"Yes. I wonder what was 'just getting better?'"

He tilted his head toward the financial reports. "When we look at those again, we may well conclude that, at the very least, Tom created some extra family income. But that could have been going on for a while."

"So why better now? You'd think…"

A hiss from under the table made me duck to look at Cat and Mister Tibbs. She had settled by Syl's feet, and Cat by mine. "Play nice, you two."

Cat sat on his haunches and stared at me, nonplussed. Then he put one paw on my foot.

"Jeez." I stood and got a few pieces of cat food from the plastic tub under the kitchen counter. Cat did not move, so I pointed to the floor near his bowl. "I'm not feeding you under the table."

From his seat at the table, Syl said, "He knows he can manipulate you, and he's hell bent on making sure you know."

"Funny." Once Cat moved away, Mister Tibbs lay down and put her head on Syl's shoe. I tilted my head toward her. "She's still not real lively. I think the fire scared her." I returned to my chair.

"I'm surprised none of those files survived."

"I forgot to tell you the sheriff said the firebug used some kind of accelerant."

"Damn. Are you sure you feel safe here?"

"I think the person got what they wanted. Ambrose is coming down one day this week, and he says he's going to put stronger locks on the windows."

"They came in a door."

I nodded. "For the door in the basement, I'm going to get one of those deadbolts that you can only open with a key from the inside, too. Then they can't break a window and just reach in to unlock it."

"And you can't get out."

"I'm going to tell myself where the key is."

He smiled and stood. "I'm not offering to do the dishes, but I'll carry some of them to the sink."

I finished my last bites of meatball and glanced at his back, as he walked the short distance to the sink. A few times I've wondered whether I might be interested in Syl, but not seriously thought about it.

For one thing, the entire time I've known him I've been reeling from one piece of bad news to another. For another, I'd guess he's at least ten to twelve years older than my twenty-eight years. Hardly prohibitive, but since I think I'd like kids someday, it's something to consider.

His voice caught me by surprise. "Penny for your thoughts?"

"Gosh. I half drifted off. I never went back to bed after the fire."

"I hadn't thought about that. We can look at these financial reports tomorrow."

I shook my head as I stood with my plate. "I'd like to hear your ideas, at least some of them. If I doze off, just take Mister Tibbs out one more time before you leave."

She barked from under the table, and her nails clicked as she walked out from under it. Cat meowed from his spot next to his food bowl.

"You've both had plenty to eat. Go play somewhere."

As I passed Cat, he reached out a paw and smacked my jeans, but he hadn't put out his claws. Then he huffed to his chair, which I'd positioned under the window, and hopped up.

As I cleared the few other things from the table, Syl placed the four annual reports side by side and put a page of notes next to them.

I rinsed tomato sauce from the plates, so it didn't harden, and stood next to him. "What do you think?"

He pointed to the one on the left. "If we take the one from six years ago as a baseline, it's clear costs went up a lot over the following years. I remember you said having one silo down should have made a decent drop in utility bills."

"Yes. Electricity for one less silo should have made a difference."

"Right. So, I checked with Southeast Iowa Electric Co-op – interesting group by the way – and utility rates during that time were almost steady."

"So, electricity costs shouldn't have gone up. Or should have gone down, with less use. Why do you find the co-op interesting?" I knew several people who either worked for it or served on its board of directors, which was a lot more formal than the now-disbanded group at the Dodson Elevator.

"We city types think of executives in suits when we think of utilities. And people on the telephone poles and such. But not an office where a couple workers are in business casual and a few others wear blue jeans."

I shrugged. "The parallel to judging a book by its cover comes to mind."

"Kind of the opposite. The deputy director I talked to invited me over, said he'd give me a couple of their annual reports. So, I stopped by when I got back from Des Moines late this afternoon. Hell of a sophisticated operation."

"Did you tell him why you wanted the reports?"

"I may be a business consultant rather than an investigator, but I know how to snoop without inviting questions."

I smiled as I picked up the second annual report he had arrayed on the table. "Wouldn't have been electricity in a lot of farm country until the 1940s or later if communities hadn't created those co-ops."

"No profit incentive to serve relatively few people," he agreed. "Half the co-op's building is solar-powered, and they're putting in a few wind turbines in the southwestern part of the county."

"Yep. More wind power further west in Iowa, but it blows down here, too." I smiled. "They rotate people on and off that board. You'll really be part of South County if you volunteer to be on it."

"Yeah, I'd be a fish out of water."

"Pretty soon you'll be just another corncob in the crib." I pointed at the summary of assets. "So, other than you are now a fan of electric co-ops, what else is new?"

"I learned what I wanted to. Dodson's utility costs should not have increased. It matters because utilities are a larger part of his costs than they would be in a firm that only uses electricity for lights and computers and such."

I nodded. "What he calls Grain Payables also went up a lot each year."

"Agreed. But Dodson's financial reports don't tell us whether he took in more grain that he's waiting for payment for, or raised the cost of processing and storage on a similar amount of grain. If it's the latter and costs didn't go up, there's a fresh bundle of profit."

"Or money to hide." I pointed at one of the reports again. "Like the bigwigs on Wall Street say, what's the bottom line?"

He half-shrugged. "If we make the very rude assumption that his costs stayed similar and he didn't show growing net income, he would have had money to skim. He could have made as much as a quarter or half a million dollars over three or four years."

"Not a lot for Wall Street, but darn good in Southeast Iowa."

He collected the paperwork and stacked it before handing the small pile to me. "That amount of untaxed income is a huge amount, even by Southern California standards."

I CALLED SANDI TUESDAY morning. "Are you obligated to tell Scott everything we talk about?"

"Who you hire to fix shingles on your house, no. Other stuff, I have to be careful. What do you have? Meet at the diner?"

I thought for a second. "No. If we get into deep conversation, somebody'll tell Scott or Ryan we had our heads together, and they'll ask what's up. Why don't you bring a camera out here?"

"And I could ask why."

"Tell them you want to see if there are any decent pictures of my charming burn barrel. Surely Scott knows the fire was set."

She said nothing for several seconds. "You know, that spot in your yard is visible from the road."

I swore, loudly. Cat raised his lazy head from his spot, and Mister Tibbs yipped.

"So, Ryan came out here and took pictures?"

"From the road."

I started to ask her, in full sarcasm mode, when we stopped confiding in each other, but remembered I'd been using Syl as a sounding board instead of her. "Too long a conversation for Hy-Vee. Aren't you working on anything with a local history angle? We could meet at the library."

"When?"

"I have to take care of the livestock and touch base with Stooper. An hour."

"Livestock? Did Ambrose buy cows or something?"

"I'll explain when I see you."

Cat showed no interest in the forty-degree morning, so Mister Tibbs and I took another stroll around the farmyard. "Okay, I know you can take care of yourself. My big decision is whether to leave you and Cat in the same area, or whether I should lock one of you in a separate room."

She peed on some wilted zinnias near the porch.

"I'll take that as you asserting yourself. Just remember, you aren't real big, but you're bigger than Cat. If he tries to smack you, bark really loud. Right in his face."

THE RIVER'S EDGE PUBLIC LIBRARY is barely 500 square feet and resides in what was a shoe store years ago. I nodded at the long-time, elderly head librarian and looked for Sandi. She sat at one of the ancient tables, the definitive volume of *Early South County History* open in front of her. The chapter facing up was "Schools and Newspapers."

I slid in across from her. "Hey."

She grinned. "Heard you got Mr. Patel's big ol' cat."

I rolled my eyes. "When we're done, I'm going home for a few minutes. I left them together rather than in separate rooms."

"That's either bold or borders on lunacy. Let me know if you still have a bedspread."

"Probably not smart, but I don't want to get into organizing their play space every day. Listen…" I leaned across the table. "I have something for you, but you can't do your screech thing."

She tossed her red ponytail. "I do not screech."

I raised my eyebrows.

"Much. What do you have?"

"It might not be anything, but you can dig into it more than I can in the next couple of days." I laid out the possibility that Dodson Elevator's expenses were made to look higher, which could have made it possible to skim money off the top.

She absorbed the information quietly. "Hard to know, isn't it? Good you had Syl to evaluate all this."

"Don't be snotty."

She shrugged. "It's a private company. What Dodson did with his money was up to him, but why not show it?"

"Two possible reasons. At least. One, he wanted to raise the price of processing and storage, and he couldn't justify it, if it became known he had great profits. Another is that he and Janet were socking away a lot of money."

"Or maybe he did it alone," Sandi said.

"I thought about that. Since she seems hard up for money, maybe he was hiding it from her, too. The thing is, an owner would need someone in finance or accounting working with them. I can't imagine he fudged all that data himself."

She brightened. "That means we can ask people besides Janet."

"My thinking exactly. I'm starting with Dad's friend, Jeb Nelson."

"We don't know who's taking over for Dodson. I'll stop by the elevator to ask about that. I was thinking about waiting until after the funeral, but a big city paper wouldn't be so polite."

After she and I feigned interest in an article on the many daily and weekly papers that had graced River's Edge doorsteps through the years, I headed back to the farm. *Too bad I can't bill Mister Tibbs and Cat for gas money.*

I'd only gone a few blocks when my cell phone rang. Caller ID showed it was the veterinary clinic. I pulled over in front of one of the downtown's vacant storefronts.

"Melanie? You were right. Someone gave her a light sedative. Actually, a pain medication."

My jaw clenched. "What? Are you sure?"

"Yes. You heard of Gabapentin? It's used for nerve pain in humans, and small doses are sometimes used for anxiety or pain in dogs. She doesn't normally take it, does she?"

"She isn't on any medication. I would get anything from you."

"My guess is your visitor used some that they had as their own prescription. No way to tell. Mister Tibbs will be okay, but it probably explains her lack of barking until something really stimulated her."

My face flushed, and I gripped the phone tightly. "It still doesn't explain why she didn't bark initially... Oh, I guess the door they came in was far from where I was sleeping."

"So, she might have growled or yipped, but if they gave her a good treat, maybe one with the medicine in it, all they had to do was sit with her for a few minutes until she calmed down."

I said nothing for several seconds.

"You there?"

"Yes. I guess I should be glad she's okay."

"And get an alarm system." He hung up.

The closer I got to home the more I seethed. How dare someone drug my dog? Did the person who broke in know I was in the house?

The dark house would have looked inviting to someone who wanted those boxes. Still, pretty bold. Maybe it was Janet Dodson and she didn't care about anything, or she was so upset she didn't think about the ramifications of finding me home.

The intruder left in a hurry when I screamed. I ran out the other side of the house, or I might have stumbled into them. I remembered the sound of a car peeling away. I'd told Gallagher about that, but by the time deputies searched the yard, tire tracks of many cars and the firetruck wove over one another.

Frenetic barks reached my ears as I drove into the yard. Either Mister Tibbs was anxious to see me, or Cat had made her life miserable for the last hour or so.

The living room implied the latter. Hands on hips, I surveyed the area. Cat's food bowl sat in the middle of the room. His chair was overturned, and Mister Tibbs sat next to it.

Cat was atop the table. Mister Tibbs could have chased Cat around the house. Or Cat could have started it and jumped on the table to avoid consequences.

I stared at each one for several seconds. "This is not how it's going to be."

Cat yawned, and I shook a finger at him. "You want to be outside all day? That can be arranged."

I righted the chair, picked up the cat bowl, shooed Cat off the table, and made for the kitchen. The dead mouse, or half of one, in the middle of that room stopped me cold. Mice often hide in homes once the weather gets cool.

Cat meowed loudly and strutted into the kitchen. He sniffed the mouse, then sat by it, expecting a reward.

"Okay, now I get it."

Mister Tibbs yipped from behind me.

"Was it a team effort, or did Cat do it all?"

She cocked her curly head at me.

I took a dog treat from the counter jar and a cat treat from the bag under the sink. "Thank you both, but you need to figure out how to chase rodents without knocking over stuff."

CHAPTER TWELVE

JEB NELSON'S PLACE IS not far from Syl's on the western side of town. It sits off a gravel road, at the end of a narrow lane that has no street sign. The lane stops at the river, with only his house at the end of its quarter-mile length. I'd seen tractors and balers use the lane to get to the huge field of hay that abuts a small copse of walnut and oak trees. Otherwise, I figured only Jeb used the lane.

I hadn't been able to find a phone number for him. While stopping by unannounced seemed rude, I had no other option. A lot of older farmers came home to eat a hot meal in the middle of the day, and this Tuesday Jeb was no exception. I smelled green beans simmering before he opened the door.

He smiled as he greeted me and stood aside to let me in. "Melanie. This is a surprise."

"Sorry to just stop by, but I couldn't find a phone number."

"I'll give it to you before you go. Got rid of the house phone, so I only have a cell phone." He led me toward an old-fashioned, red Formica-topped kitchen table that fit the tiny cottage to a T.

When we sat opposite across the table and I had refused his offer of coffee, I said, "Since you were at the dinner, you know I found Tom Dodson."

He nodded. "Sorry you had to see that."

"I don't think he…suffered much."

His eyes smiled. "And you've heard that your father and I butted heads with him about a few things, and came by to see if I did it."

"No, of course not." I stopped. "Oh, you're kidding."

"'Course I am. Besides, I moved my processing and storage to Hopewell a couple years ago, because I thought Dodson was charging too much. And was getting to be a real pain in the tailbone."

"You think Ambrose and I should do that next year?"

"I'd get quotes from both of them, but that's just me."

I nodded. "Good idea. I know you and Dad were on that advisory board at the elevator."

"Not that Dodson took much advice."

"And it's since been dissolved, right?"

Nelson shrugged. "Not sure Tom would have put it that way, but yes. He could run the place however he wanted."

"Yes. You still interested in the place becoming a co-op?"

"Could be. Depends what Janet wants to do. I'm afraid she'll sell to one of those CAFO places, and they'll raise rates even higher."

That surprised me. "You don't hear as much about the consolidated agricultural food operations, not since South County passed those ordinances about processing animal waste."

"True. It raised CAFO operating costs, so they aren't as quick to buy up land for the big hog and chicken lots."

I was happy because their so-called by-products were stinky, especially on hot days.

"Still," Nelson said, "occasionally a CAFO will buy an elevator to keep their feed costs lower."

"So, are you going to lead a group to set up a co-op?"

He frowned. "I'm seventy-five, good bit older than your dad was. If some of the younger families want to take the lead, I'll support them. And participate."

"Good to hear." I paused, not sure how to phrase my next question. "Look, this is going to sound stupid, but did you ever hear anything about my parents' car accident?"

He had been leaning his arms on the table, but now sat back and folded them. "Some talk about bad brakes and things back then. No proof of anything. And it was a lousy night. Not sure I would have driven on the highway, what with sleet coming. Not that I'm criticizing your parents for heading out."

I smiled, thinking of my father. "I asked Dad about the weather. He was convinced the bad stuff wouldn't start until closer to dawn."

His eyebrows went up, then down, and he shut his eyes for a moment. "I'm glad to hear you say that. I wished I'd talked to the son-of-a-gun about it. At least, I know someone did."

"He wasn't overly stubborn, but when he made up his mind, it was usually hard to change. So, uh, you don't think anyone say, monkeyed around with their car?"

He seemed to choose his words carefully. "The fire was so bad, it was impossible to tell. Truck driver they ran into thought he saw another car passing them right before they hit the semi. Could have made your Dad swerve, but there were no suspects about who would deliberately force him out of his lane. And not stop."

I had heard mention about another vehicle in the area, but not that someone left without helping my parents. Or if I had heard it during the first few weeks, I'd forgotten it.

The remnants of my reporter skills weren't willing to let go just yet. "Do you know if Dad argued with Tom Dodson about GMO seed stuff, or confronted him about whether he'd been padding costs to take money out of the business?"

He shrugged. "GMO seed was a bigger topic a few years ago than now, but I don't recall your dad saying he argued with Dodson about it."

So, did Dodson bring up the GMO point to steer me away from his finances?

Nelson frowned. "Embezzling? We talked about why prices went up when costs should have been going down. But," he sounded bitter, "Dodson was devious when he wanted to be, but I'm not sure how anyone would prove embezzling now. And why would Tom do that? It was his company. He could pay himself whatever he wanted and report it accurately."

I shrugged. "Avoid taxes? I might have a starting point. The question is, do I have any business pursuing it? Who gets hurt?" I told him about the burn barrel fire. "My concern is that whoever started it was after the financial statements."

"Heard about the fire from the Donovans. We got our flu shots at the senior center this morning." He smiled. "Not as good as whatever Shirley dishes out at the diner, but always a good place to catch up on goings-on around town."

I grimaced. "The story was too late for the Monday paper. Probably be in the Wednesday *South County News,* and then everybody'll know about it."

"Hmm. You having those profit and loss statements is useful, but they're dated. 'Course, if Janet sells the business, she'll have to get an outside firm to swear to its soundness. They'll go over every inch of the company's finances. Same as when you sell a farm."

I nodded. "They want to know what the land can bring, not just how much of it you have to sell."

He regarded me. "You going to pursue this?"

I didn't say mostly because I was furious about Mister Tibbs being drugged. "I'll talk to a few more people. But not in the next few days. I want Janet and her daughter to get through the funeral."

He stood. "You be careful what you stir up."

BY MID-AFTERNOON, I HAD the decorative cabbage plants and met Stooper on the square to plant them in the large pots in front of the variety store and pharmacy.

Stooper finished patting the plant into place at the pharmacy. "Mel, you're charging only $25 for this? It's not enough."

I almost said he would still get paid his usual rate, but decided his comment had nothing to do with that. "It's mostly for marketing. Mr. Patel and the pharmacist have said people asked about them, and the Chamber called to see if we could do theirs again next spring."

"Be really good if the guy who runs the Chamber gets us to take care of his lawn. He has almost an acre."

I picked up the two trowels from the sidewalk and opened the back of my pickup. "I'm working on a letter to send to about ten homes."

"Why not more?"

"Because I'm an optimist." I laughed at his puzzled expression. "We can only do so many houses. Suppose six of them hire us?"

He sat on the edge of the planter. "We can hire someone else to help."

I nodded. "True. If we don't get a lot of calls for estimates, I'll send out a bunch more."

"Good. Not enough people dyin' in this town. I don't get as much headstone business as I used to."

"Surprises me. I guess the population is pretty static, but it's older."

He stood. "Yeah, but a lot more of 'em are getting cremated. Don't need headstones."

I hadn't thought about that. Essentially my parents were. Ambrose and I had their few remains placed in one cremated remains urn and erected a memorial stone in the local cemetery. I couldn't imagine not having a place to put flowers on Memorial Day.

"Tell you what, Stooper. I'll get some flyers printed up. You can visit a few people you know in person."

He pushed his ball cap back on his head. "Maybe I'll get Syl to suggest folks."

"He hardly knows anyone." Seeing Stooper's dejected expression, I added, "Maybe he'll let us put one of those signs in his yard in the spring. You know, landscaping by…" I stopped. I hadn't picked a name.

Stooper laughed. "You didn't like the names I gave you. Now you need one for your cat."

I SAT IN MASON'S DINER making two lists. The one with names for my landscaping business was blank.

The second had ideas for how people could hide money other than burying it in their back yard. Nothing about Tom Dodson led me to think he had the sophistication to create offshore accounts in some tax haven.

Before digitized financial systems, a person could set up a bank account in another state and figure their cash wasn't easily findable. Not so today.

What about using a false Social Security number to open an account? It wouldn't matter if Tom Dodson had done that. I had no way to learn about it.

He could have hidden it in something collectible, like coins or baseball cards. Some people who ran Ponzi schemes gave away substantial sums to charity, but I'd never heard of Tom Dodson being especially generous.

I didn't know a lot about Bitcoin or other non-bank ways of storing and transferring assets. I doubted Tom would have used them.

None of these options helped me figure out if Tom Dodson had a lot of extra money. Knowing he had substantial assets would simply reinforce Syl's and my thinking about his financial reports. But even if he did skim funds from his own company, the malfeasance likely didn't have anything to do with his murder. Or did it?

Why did I care? Because someone had broken into my house, drugged Mister Tibbs, and burned a bunch of my father's files. Someone with a vested interest in Dodson Grain Elevator wanted to be sure I didn't learn how much money came in and went out.

My phone chirped, but the caller's name did not appear. "Hello?"

Ryan's voice was firm. "So, Melanie, I know you don't want to talk to me, but I have a couple of questions."

"You've got pictures of the burn barrel after the fire."

He said nothing.

"I told Sandi she could come out and take some. She ratted you out."

"I stayed on the road."

I kept my tone cool. "So she told me."

"I wondered if you took any pictures during the fire?"

"Like if I used my phone camera after I called 9-1-1?"

He sounded excited. "Exactly."

"No. Ryan, I'm busy."

"I saw your car at Mason's Diner. You're taking a break."

"A working break. I'm hanging up."

"Mel, one question. Mrs. Keyser said you picked up the boxes at her house. What was in them?"

I considered for a second. Better to say something innocuous. "My family's records about the farm and some pictures. Gotta go." I hung up.

I drummed my fingers on the table for a minute and then called Mrs. Keyser.

She answered just before I was about to hang up. "Hello Melanie. I was in the little girls' room."

Can there be an appropriate response to that? "Sorry if I got you away from there."

"Are you recovered from the fire behind your house?"

Translated: *Tell me more.*

"Could have been a lot worse. No damage to the house."

"Goodness. But someone broke in to get those boxes of files. I still can't believe it."

I envisioned her in a bright-colored house coat, sinking into the couch for a good chat. I was not in the mood. "I wanted to talk to you about those boxes."

"Do tell."

"Uh, it's just I kind of wish you wouldn't. I don't think the town needs to know what was in the boxes that were burned."

Silence.

Her tone grew formal. "I see."

Great. She's told a dozen people.

When she said nothing else, I added, "It was really my father's business what he kept, and I'd just as soon leave it that way."

"I understand completely."

I didn't need her to admit that she blabbed, and I wanted off the phone. "So, are you ready for Halloween?"

"And you with a black cat. Make sure you don't let it run around outside before Halloween."

"Don't think we have any kitty-nappers out my way. I'll talk to you another time."

As I hung up, it occurred to me that Ryan could have been sitting next to her on the couch.

I SPENT AN HOUR Tuesday, just before dark, decorating the house for Halloween, which was only a few days away. Mostly I carved a couple of pumpkins and added black and orange streamers to the outside porch rail in the front. I didn't do it at the side doors because they weren't easily seen from the road.

Tom Dodson's funeral was the next morning, so I planned to avoid discussing his demise until at least Thursday. As it got dark, I worked for an hour on business flyers Stooper and I could distribute. I'd have to buy a printer. And think of a name for the business.

The house phone startled me. "Melanie. Sheriff Gallagher here."

"Hi. Any news?"

"Only that you've talked to Mrs. Keyser about who she gossiped to about your dad's files."

I thought fast. "I don't want her blabbing about my family's business. In fact, I called her because I gathered she had talked to Ryan. Or someone she talked to had talked to him."

"I appreciate that. But I need you to promise me, again, not to poke into Tom Dodson's murder."

"I found out why Mister Tibbs didn't bark." I told him about the veterinarian's discovery of Gabapentin in her system.

Mister Tibbs yipped, as if reinforcing what I said.

"The pain medicine?"

"Doc Marshall said it can be used for pain or as a mild sedative for dogs."

"Crud." Gallagher said nothing for a few more seconds, then added, "I don't like this."

"Me either, but the person got what they wanted. The files are gone."

"If that's all they wanted. You keep a phone by your bed?"

"Yes." When he said nothing else, I added, "I thought of one more thing from, you know, after the Farm Bureau dinner."

"What's that?"

"Right after Janet knelt next to Tom, she said something like, 'Things were just getting better.'"

Gallagher grew stern. "Why the hell didn't you tell me that Saturday?"

"Because I'd just found a body and had a bloody handprint on my shirt."

"Fair enough. Let's go back to the break-in. You're convinced the person didn't steal anything else?"

"You were in here. The most valuable thing I own is the antique pie safe."

"I like this situation less every day. If you don't want to buy a full security system, get some of those devices to put on window sashes. They screech if someone tries to come in."

"Are there any for doors?"

"Google it," he said. "Anything else?"

"I don't think so. If I remember something I'll call you."
"I noticed you didn't make that promise." He hung up.

CHAPTER THIRTEEN

MY PHONE RANG AS I climbed into bed. "Who would call at ten o'clock on a Tuesday night?"

Mister Tibbs' yip said she had no idea.

Syl sounded chipper. "You still up?"

My heart beat faster. Probably the surprise of the call. "Just getting into bed. What's up?"

His tone grew more serious. "Just thought we'd go over those financial reports some more."

"Ah. Are you in town tomorrow?"

"Working in my home office. Meet for lunch or coffee?"

"Sure. You want to call me? I'll be around town, but I'll have my phone."

"You call me. Talk to you tomorrow."

Something to look forward to.

WEDNESDAY MORNING BROUGHT COLDER air, with no sign of rain. I had errands to run and leaf raking to do at Mrs. Keyser's. She gave me reduced rent because I mowed and trimmed her lawn. When I moved, I told her I would do whatever fall maintenance she needed. Her lawn and gardens had improved so much under my care that people often asked her who did the work. Better than an ad in the paper.

As I drove toward town at seven-thirty, my thoughts turned to the *South County News*. A new issue would be out today, if not already. I hoped it didn't mention the burn barrel fire too prominently.

No such luck.

"Rural Fire May be Linked to Farm Bureau Murder."

Nothing subtle about that headline. I scowled as I put coins into the newspaper box in front of the pharmacy and walked into the diner with the paper.

The article darkened my mood, already gloomy the more I thought about someone drugging Mister Tibbs.

>Firefighters were called to the farm owned by Ambrose and Melanie Perkins at 3 a.m. Monday to quash a fire in the burn barrel behind the house. Suspicion of arson was raised from the start, because the barrel had not been in use and firefighters smelled gasoline.
>
>After the fire was doused, the barrel was found to contain remnants of files that had once belonged to the Perkins' siblings' parents, Arnold and Martha, who perished in a multi-vehicle accident three years ago.
>
>Some of the destroyed material dealt with the senior Perkins' role as an advisory board member for Dodson Grain Elevator, whose owner, Tom Dodson, was murdered Saturday night near the community room of the local Methodist Church. Dodson had abolished the advisory group shortly after Arnold Perkins' death.
>
>Since no one has read the files for years, except possibly Melanie Perkins, it cannot be known whether they held proprietary information about grain elevator operations.
>
>Melanie Perkins had brought the files to the farm only Sunday afternoon. When pressed about why

someone would break into the Perkins' home to steal and burn the files, Sheriff Gallagher had no comment.

Fire Chief Dan Thomas said, "While the only damage to the house was singed shingles at the back, the fire was a serious incident. Had the wind been stronger or Ms. Perkins' dog not awakened her, we could be having a very different conversation today."

Efforts to follow up with South County Sheriff Gallagher about finding Dodson's killer were not successful. As of press time, all that was known was Dodson died after sustaining a blow to the head.

Ryan's byline. Bile rose in my throat. He wrote about the role of the advisory group and that Dodson had abolished it soon after my father's death. Ryan had no business mentioning anything about my parents or implying something could have been in the files relating to Dodson's murder.

Since Ryan hadn't interviewed me, his information had to have come from Mrs. Keyser. *I bet he was sitting next to her when I called.*

Good old Hal said smelly facts sold newspapers. Ryan had learned well. He sensationalized where Sandi and I would have stuck to facts.

I reread the article. It prompted me to wonder again why the person bothered to burn the files rather than simply steal them.

An enraged or crazed person might not have been thinking clearly. On the other hand, the boxes of files would have been hard to hide.

If Janet broke in, she might have gotten them into her home before her daughter or others came to town to be with her, but family members look around after someone dies. Not necessarily to be nosy, but to see if things need to be moved or given away.

Files about the elevator, even with my dad's notes, wouldn't arouse suspicion. But paperwork about our farm operations would raise questions. And if she placed them in another business's dumpster, someone might find them.

I went back to the idea that whoever burned the files should have clothing that smelled like smoke and, perhaps, sooty shoes. I grinned. Instead of a smoking gun, smoky clothes.

"Shug, are you losing your mind?"

I grinned at Shirley as she placed a coffee cup in front of me. "Just amusing myself. What do you hear?"

"Nothing. Probably be people coming in after the funeral. You going?"

I had no intention of attending Tom Dodson's funeral, but I would abide by the common practice of signing the guest book at the funeral home beforehand. I said so.

Shirley shook her head and adjusted her apron. "Poor Janet. To have that article appear today." She studied me, likely looking for a reaction.

"You hear anyone talking about it?"

She glanced around the booths. "Don't see a lot of folks here, do you?"

"Wonder why not?"

She shrugged. "Big funeral. People have to change their patterns."

At the sound of the diner's door opening, she turned toward the arriving pharmacist. "You want that usual cup of joe to go?"

Dodson's service was at ten. After my bagel and coffee, I drove to the Eternal Tranquility Funeral Home to be there when their doors opened at eight-thirty.

I smiled as I walked toward the entrance. The original owners had the last names of Edwards and Thompson. They figured the odds of anyone in their families continuing in the business were not great, so they used their initials as the first letters of the name they chose.

Eternal Tranquility, whose current owners are named Ruben and Summers, has two large funeral chapels and two smaller rooms. The business created the small areas a few years ago. People who had outlived all their friends could have a respectful viewing area, but their families or estates didn't have to pay for a large room with a chapel.

I thought of it as a kind idea and had written a short piece about it for the paper. The photo I'd taken of one of the newer rooms showed a space smaller than most living rooms, but with the traditional funeral home décor – plush carpets, dark wood, and understated wallpaper.

My plan today was to zip in and out, leaving a card in a slot behind where the guest book was situated. I nodded at the ancient Mrs. Appleby, who sits at a desk near the funeral home entrance, and she pointed to the largest chapel, which was to the right of the foyer.

I stopped at the edge of the space. Sitting in one of the upholstered chairs in the vestibule immediately outside the chapel entrance was a petite, blonde woman in an almost elegant navy-blue dress with white piping. Dressed for a funeral, but not in black, and dabbing her eyes.

I debated stepping out of the room. She must have heard me, because she said, "I'm sorry. Please don't leave."

The voice was familiar, and I pasted on a formal-type smile as I turned back. I recognized Ginny Forman as the relatively new assistant librarian. She'd been in town a while, but I didn't know where she had worked prior to the library.

"Hi, Ginny. I don't mind coming back later."

She nodded at the sealed envelope I carried. "I brought a card, too. I'm not coming to the service, so I thought I'd stop by."

I quickly signed my name and address, as is customary, and picked up the short program. Tom Dodson's smiling face graced the front page, along with his name and dates of birth and death. I stuffed it into my purse to read the tribute later.

"I'll walk out with you," Ginny said.

We bade Mrs. Appleby goodbye and blinked our way into the bright October sunshine.

"I visited my parents over the weekend, so I didn't hear about his death until Monday. Quite a shock."

"Yes, a big shock."

Ginny stopped abruptly. "Oh dear, I just remembered that you're the one who found him at the Farm Bureau meeting. I'm sure that was difficult."

"Very. I wish I could have helped him."

Our vehicles were near each other in the large lot. We walked the short distance in silence. I broke it. "You moved here a few years ago, right?"

"I moved into town then. I grew up about fifteen miles north of River's Edge, a few miles from Fairfield."

We reached her gold, late model Camry. Very classy. "Do you enjoy working at the library?"

"A great deal. I've been able to add to the children's collection. Good to get them started reading early. You do, uh, landscaping work?"

I grinned. "After Hal Morris canned me from the paper."

Her mouth turned down. "Oh, my. You found him, too."

I keep Hal's death in one corner of my mind. I can joke about his writing with Sandi or ruminate about his temper without thinking of finding his body. Most people only associate me with the latter.

"Yes. Also not a good day." She looked as if she might cry, so I asked, "What did you do before you worked at the library?"

"I was the accounting assistant at Dodson Elevator. That's how I know, knew, Tom."

Bingo.

"Gosh. You knew him well. I'm sorry." My mind formulated questions about the issues Syl saw in the profit and loss statements, but luckily a judgment gene kept me from blurting them. Today, anyway.

She hesitated, and squared her shoulders, "For a time, yes. I, uh, have to work during the funeral, so I stopped by on the way."

I pushed a button on my key fob to unlock my pickup. "I'll see you in the library sometime."

She nodded as she got into her car and almost peeled out of the parking lot.

A memory flitted about my brain, but I couldn't quite nab it. I didn't know Ginny beyond the grocery store and library, and I couldn't remember running into her the few times I'd gone to the elevator office for a story or to drop off a check for my dad.

What was it? As my truck swung into the law enforcement parking lot, thoughts came together. I'd covered a book signing for a children's author, who had been gracious enough to put our small-town library on her promotional tour. Tom Dodson stopped by the event.

His presence didn't seem odd. Dodson Elevator was a library foundation patron, as were half the businesses in town. Bruce Blackner had been there bragging about the fact that his daughter was about to give him his first grandchild – though he didn't know then it would be twins – and even Doc Shelton had come for a few minutes.

Dodson never struck me as the bookish type. My guess would be he attended to support his former staff member more than the library. How well did he know her?

How snarky can I get? Still, I couldn't help but think she might have known something about how he spent company funds. Maybe some even paid for that expensive car.

Very snarky.

CHAPTER FOURTEEN

I DID SOME BOOKKEEPING WORK and visited a nursery near Keosauqua to pick up a few dozen spring bulbs to plant around the farmhouse. If I landscaped the area around the house really well it could advertise my business. Except I still needed a name.

As I came back into River's Edge, almost on a whim, I drove by Dodson Grain Elevator on the edge of town. A sign had been erected with Tom's name, dates of birth and death, and the words **Closed in Mourning Today**.

The office had several rooms and a limestone cellar. I always assumed it had been converted from a farmhouse. It would have been called a ramshackle building if the Dodsons hadn't kept it painted and planted a few flowers around it. Today it had a forlorn look.

Feeling at loose ends, at lunchtime I returned to Mason's Diner and called Syl. I wished I'd thought to call earlier, but he said he'd meet me at the diner in twenty minutes. I didn't say I was already here.

The sparse clientele reminded me that a lot of people in town would have gone not only to Tom Dodson's funeral but the dinner afterwards. The crowd was so small that, after she placed my order for tomato soup and a BLT, Shirley sat across from me in the booth.

She refastened a pin that kept her thin hairnet in place. "Hear anything around town this morning, Shug?"

"If you mean about Tom, you've probably heard more."

"Still not hardly anything. People talk about how someone must have snuck into the church, killed him, and left fast."

I studied her, half amused. "As opposed to someone else who attended the dinner?"

She shrugged. "Not to be gross, but wouldn't a killer have maybe had some blood on them?"

"I don't know. I think the injury was to the back of his head. I know the scalp bleeds a lot. But I think of a person's torso as spurting more blood than the skull. Maybe the blood ran down the back of Dodson's head."

I watched Shirley mentally file away my thought, but all she said was, "Ugh."

I didn't really know that. I'd have to ask Doc Shelton or better yet the ME, Dr. MacGregor. He's head of pathology and hematology at the hospital, but in a small county that made him most qualified to determine cause of death. Nothing in the paper had mentioned the autopsy results. Maybe Sandi knew.

"Seems if he had been injured not long before I found him, I might have seen his killer in the hallway."

"Or bathroom," Shirley offered. "You know, if it was a she-type person."

I smiled. "True. I suppose we usually think of men as the killers."

"But who would kill the guy? He could be a loudmouth, but…" She gestured around the room, "I never saw him argue with anyone in here. Not even politics and stuff."

I shrugged. "A lot of arguments are private. Or in business meetings."

Shirley raised her eyebrows and gave me a sly smile. "Or in the bedroom?"

"Really? What have you heard?"

"Nothing specific. But I'd say he seemed a lot happier the last year or so." She frowned. "Until lately. Well, not especially unhappy recently. Maybe more serious."

"Hmm." After a couple of seconds, I said, "I think Janet was in the community room with about a hundred other people, so her time isn't in question."

"No, but if he was fooling around, maybe she had somebody whack him."

I laughed loudly, and an older couple seated at the diner's lunch counter turned to stare at me. "Sorry, folks."

They turned back to their lunch, and I shook my head slightly at Shirley. "Do you know something, or are you sowing thoughts to see what grows?"

"Bit of both. If he'da been a better tipper, I wouldn't look for stories." She nodded toward the pass-through counter in front of the kitchen and stood. "I'll get your sandwich."

She stopped to take an order en route to my BLT, so I turned over the conversation. I knew nothing of Tom and Janet's marriage, nor did I care to. Since her whereabouts that night were known, if a killer had something to do with a love triangle, Janet was off the hook for direct action.

What if Tom's happiness Shirley talked about was the first blush of an affair, and the more serious appearance later marked the end of one? Would a spurned lover care enough to kill Tom?

Financially he'd be a good catch. Or he might lose a lot in a divorce. Even if he didn't, stealing a spouse created a lot of problems for the honeybunch, not the least of which would be a tarnished local reputation.

I almost regretted my decision not to poke around until after the funeral. Then I remembered most people who could have information would attend it, so I'd be wasting my time.

Sandi slid into the booth across from me. "Called your cell, and you didn't answer. Mad about the article?"

Since Syl was about to join me, I wasn't pleased to see her. I pulled the phone from my pocket and saw an unanswered call. "Not at you. Guess I was in a dead spot between here and Keosauqua."

Sandi nodded at Shirley, who would recognize that meant she wanted a cup of tea. "You know," Sandi said, "if you don't like the reporting, you should apply for the editor's job."

I snorted. "No way. Besides, the time to apply ended a few weeks ago, right?"

She nodded. "I don't think Doc Shelton and the rest of the committee like the applicants."

That surprised me. Newspaper jobs, especially top positions, were few and far between in Southeast Iowa. "And Scott doesn't want to stay?"

"No way. You know he only came as a favor to Doc Shelton. He and his wife want to get back up to Iowa City."

"Not interested. Did you apply?" She hadn't mentioned it to me.

She shook her head. "Don't want the long hours."

I regarded her for a second, and she looked away. Maybe she had a new boyfriend. Sandi rarely spoke about her love life. "You were looking for me for something besides a career discussion. What's up?"

"I went by the grain elevator..."

"And it's closed," I threw in.

She nodded. "As are a bunch of businesses. Good old Andy's at the hardware store. His boss went to the funeral." She grimaced. "I had to listen to him mouth off about how they should have closed the store so he could."

"He just wanted food from the dinner."

"Probably. When he was done with that, he expounded on how you almost certainly killed Dodson."

My face flushed.

Sandi grinned. "And then he remembered who he was talking to and said that was the talk around town, but of course he didn't believe it."

I laughed. "He's such a moron."

She grew serious. "We haven't talked about how anyone got a weapon into the church."

"Or got it out of there."

Sandi nodded. "Meet me in the coat closet, so I can murder you during boring Farm Bureau speeches."

I glanced at the time on my cell phone. Syl should be here any minute. "I have to get some cat food and get busy at the house."

"Doing what?"

"For starters, figuring out what furniture I want. But I also need to do some brush cleanup around the burn barrel."

"You, uh, need help?"

I grinned at her perfectly painted fingernails and held up my short ones. "Nope."

The door jingled, and I waved to Syl.

Sandi's face flushed, and she lowered her voice. "Oh my God. Do you have a date?"

I moved over so Syl could sit next to me. When I glanced toward him, he slipped folded papers into his trouser pocket.

"Nope."

Syl slid in on my side of the booth. "Joining us for lunch, Sandi?"

"No. I ordered a cup of tea to go."

Shirley had been en route to us with Sandi's tea, and she turned on her heel and walked toward the kitchen, likely to get a to-go cup. Good old Shirley.

I said goodbye to Sandi and turned to Syl. "I'll move over to sit across from you."

"Stay here. You can see the paperwork better."

I wanted to say he was a bit too close for comfort. *Why did I think that?* "Good idea."

Shirley, having finished giving Sandi a to-go cup, came to our booth. "Okay, Mister Syl. Special today is fresh-made chicken noodle soup and chicken salad on wheat."

"Sounds good," he said.

I winked at Shirley. I should have waited to order my food, and she had thought of something quick to bring Syl, so my food wouldn't get cold.

"You ordering?" he asked me.

"Did just before you walked in."

Shirley moved away, and he spread out three reports. "Keeping in mind that I don't know squat about grain elevators." He lowered his voice. "I think our buddy may have embezzled more than we thought."

My eyes widened as I looked at penciled-in numbers down the side of each report. "What did you find out?"

"I can't compare costs like grain storage, but I do know how to research insurance rates." He pointed to the numbers on Dodson's profit and loss statements, noting the numbers next to them were more typical amounts to insure a business of Dodson Elevator's size.

I didn't want to burst his bubble, but didn't think all businesses were equal. "Can you, uh, compare a grain elevator to a big shoe store?"

He turned his head toward me and then looked back at the papers. "You underestimate me, Miss." He grinned. "Given that I'm examining data for a number of insurance firms, it was pretty easy to find similar-sized elevators in other towns. I'd say these numbers are about $60,000 more per year than some of the others."

"So, either he deliberately overstated expenses, or he was such a bad business owner that he didn't get any estimates..."

"Or someone in town was screwing him over," Syl said.

Shirley plopped soup in front of each of us. "Now, Mr. Syl, you're going to have to elaborate on a statement like that."

He grinned at her. "Trying to get me to fix you up with someone?"

Shirley turned so red that I'd have been worried, if she hadn't been able to scamper away so quickly.

Syl frowned. "Was I out of line? She kids around with me."

"Oh, no. But she'll repeat that story all over town." When he kept frowning, I added, "No one will know what we were talking about."

"Great. Now what?"

"I wish I knew. We're adding up numbers like crazy. The question is, what was he doing with the money?"

Shirley brought our sandwiches, and I moved to sit opposite Syl. "Thanks, Shirley. Soup was good."

When she moved away, Syl said, "My chicken was *really* good."

I glanced toward Shirley to be sure she had gotten out of hearing range. "I have some thoughts, but they're pure speculation and maybe kind of mean." I told him first about Tom promising Brenda Chase the secretary position – minus the work – and that she seemed enamored with him at the Farm Bureau dinner. "Maybe he wined and dined her."

Syl frowned. "Kind of thin."

"I agree, but she may not have been the only one. My neighbor said maybe Brenda was Tom's 'bed buddy.' Makes me think he had a reputation for being unfaithful."

Syl grinned. "You don't hear that expression too often."

"Okay, think about this. He had to have help hiding income or overstating expenses. I saw his former accountant, Ginny Forman, at the funeral home. Her grief seemed like more than that for a boss. Plus, her car is more than what a junior-level librarian could buy. Maybe she helped him embezzle, and he paid her off."

Syl chewed his sandwich for several seconds. "Could make sense. Also could have made his wife furious."

I shook my head. "Her time is accounted for."

"These guys who cheat on their wives usually move from woman to woman."

"But the Farm Bureau Dinner? Why would a lover be there?"

"A lot of people were in that room," Syl said.

I nodded. "True, but I didn't see anyone else in the hallway, and I bet the sheriff has accounted for who was where in the few minutes before I found Tom. My money's on someone coming in from the outside."

Syl looked skeptical. "And they happened on him just then?"

I was warming to my idea. "He was in the coat closet, remember?"

"I do believe I found you in that very closet."

"True. But I went there because I saw him move. He didn't have a coat there. What if he told someone to meet him there for a couple of minutes?"

"Still gets back to why."

I shrugged. "Do we care? The person arrived mad or got mad at him and hit him with a lot of force."

"With a weapon they found lying around a church basement and managed to take with them, even if it was dripping blood?"

I sighed. "I know. That's the hardest part. If this were a mystery book, I'd figure the person brought a knife and a bag to carry it out in."

We ate without speaking for a minute. Then Syl said, "Well, I worked out that he probably stole or hid, whatever you call it, even more than we thought. You, partner, need to determine who, how, and where the money went."

Partner?

MY GOOD MOOD FROM SYL referring to me as 'partner' soured when I stopped by Hy-Vee for cat food, litter, and milk.

A warbly woman's voice called, "Melanie. I'm surprised to see you here." Eliza Wright pushed a grocery cart containing only a can of soup.

"Hello, Eliza. Pretty full cart there."

Her intent gaze indicated she would not be deterred. "I'm surprised you aren't at Tom Dodson's funeral."

115

As if that's your business. "Could be the same reason you aren't. I didn't really know Tom that well. And I thought it would be easier for Janet and her daughter not to see the woman who found Tom that night."

She leaned across the handle of her cart. "I don't think Janet and her daughter will be the only two women in town missing him."

I pulled a bag of dry cat food off the shelf. "Seems as if you could wait until at least the day after the funeral before starting a rumor."

Her mouth opened and shut very fast. "I was simply pointing out that he would be missed."

"Uh-huh." I moved away a few feet, then Mister Tibbs' image crossed my mind. "Any thoughts on a particular woman?"

She literally huffed. "Wouldn't you like to know?"

"You're right. I don't need to know."

Keeping her mouth shut when someone seemed uninterested appeared to be too much of a challenge for Eliza. "You might think about who left the company. I hear Janet Dodson insisted on some changes."

I didn't want to respond, so I stared at Eliza until she dropped her eyes.

CHAPTER FIFTEEN

I LOADED THE FOOD AND milk into the front seat of my pickup, still wondering whether Janet had insisted that Ginny Forman leave the Dodson business. If she had, I could see her as Ginny's target more than Tom. However, the idea of the quiet librarian killing anyone seemed absurd.

Still, if Tom was what crime reporters might call a serial womanizer, he may have paid a high price for his behavior.

I was beginning to feel sorry for Janet Dodson.

My thoughts turned to a weapon. In a home, the proverbial fire poker might be nearby, but what would have been in the church basement?

Why not look myself? I thought Tom Dodson's funeral was scheduled for the Presbyterian Church, which was on the opposite side of town from my Methodist Church. Its parking lot, which held only one car, confirmed he wasn't being remembered in death at the same place where he died.

I parked and walked to the side door of the church. It led to a split foyer of sorts, with a few steps up to get into the main church and a much longer flight into the basement. In addition to the community room and two classrooms for Sunday school, the church office was in the basement. I figured the lone car belonged to the secretary, who worked two to three hours each day.

The locked side door featured a yellow sticky note that said **Ring bell for entry**. I did.

A woman's voice asked, "Who is it please?"

"Hi, Mrs. Reilly. It's Melanie. Do you have a lost and found?"

"Sure do." The door buzzed.

I pulled it shut, after I entered, and moved silently down the stairs. I figured I had less than a minute before Mrs. Reilly stuck her head out of the office to look for me.

The base of the stairs led to a carpeted hallway that ended in a T. To the left were the office, classrooms, and a small meeting room. To the right were restrooms, the closet in which I found Tom, and the community room.

More important, along the hallway I was in were doors labeled storage, cleaning supplies, and furnace. The furnace room and storage space were locked, but the door marked cleaning supplies was not.

I took in the several metal shelves along the left wall. They held bottles of Pine-Sol, paper towels and toilet paper, disinfectant spray, and more. A wash bucket and sink were on the wall opposite the door, and next to the sink was a sturdy-looking deep set of shelves with tools and small equipment such as drills and what I thought was an electric screwdriver.

I stood on my tiptoes. No sign of a hammer or anything easily weaponized.

To the right sat a work bench less than three feet in length, and on it was the trunk of a statue I recognized as St. Francis, its separate head, and a couple of tubes of fix-all glue and craft plaster.

Mrs. Reilly's voice came from her office door. "Melanie?"

I pictured her, short and always in a cardigan, and soundlessly shut the cleaning supply room door. What excuse could I give for taking more than a minute to get to her? As I turned the corner and smiled at her, I hit on one.

"Sorry, Mrs. Reilly. I had forgotten how close I would be to that closet. I almost went back up."

Her expression changed from suspicious to sympathetic. "You poor dear, of course. Come on, I'll show you the pile of lost stuff."

I smiled. "Same as the found stuff?"

She grinned. "Yep. What did you lose?"

"I had a brown sweater with me last Saturday, and I didn't think to take it home with me."

She grew somber. "That was a heck of a thing. Kind of makes me nervous to be down here alone. I called Sheriff Gallagher yesterday to see if he caught anyone."

"I haven't heard that he did."

She shook her head. "That's what he told me." She unlocked the door to one of the classrooms. "Big closet in the back has school supplies and lost and found."

I took in the colorful wall posters and boxes of crayons stacked neatly on a teacher's desk. Still, it was extra school. I had never wanted to attend any school on Sunday, and my parents didn't make me, except in December. They wanted me to be in the children's Christmas Eve play.

Mrs. Reilly walked ahead of me into the closet and flipped a light switch. "Hmm. You'd think it would be on top." She searched through gloves, winter hats, a slinky, and a bunch of sweaters. "Don't see it. You want to look?"

I shook my head. "I rode in with friends. I'll ask them to check their truck."

She flipped off the light. "You came with that new man. Sylvester Seaton, isn't that his name?"

Great. "He goes by Syl. I thought it would be a good way for him to meet people. He works in Des Moines and doesn't get around town much."

As we walked toward her office, Mrs. Reilly said, "I heard they sat him next to the high school principal." Her voice got lower. "But I don't think he called her yet."

My hands were at my sides. I pinched my thigh so I wouldn't laugh. "I haven't heard one way or the other."

We paused outside her office. "You getting things cleaned up after that fire?"

I nodded. "It was only in the burn barrel."

She shook her head. "So many pranksters out and about around Halloween."

Pranksters who break into people's houses for kindling?

SINCE RAIN THREATENED and Mister Tibbs needed a walk, I headed to the farm. As I drove, I pictured the shelves of tools in the cleaning supply room. I thought there had been a dark-colored tool chest on the next-to-the-bottom shelf. Anything could be in there.

I had no way to know if the cleaning supply door was usually locked. If one door was left unlocked, it would be the one that held stuff to clean up messes.

My mind traveled to the statue on the work bench. The sculpture, which was really too fancy a word for it, stood only about three feet tall. In summer it sat in the church's back garden. If its head had come off the weekend of the Farm Bureau dinner, surely someone would have related the separation to the murder. But it seemed too heavy to have been easily wielded as a murder weapon.

The sheriff would surely have checked the statue for blood or whatever. "Ugh."

A couple of rogue raindrops hit the windshield as I pulled into the yard, so I hustled in with the litter and food. Mister Tibbs and Cat hadn't torn the place apart in my absence, a good sign.

I whistled and called, "Come on, girl."

A yawning Mister Tibbs came out of my bedroom, and Cat hopped down from his chair. It seemed they had staked out their territories.

Cat stayed on the porch, while I half jogged around the house with Mister Tibbs. I slowed, so Mister Tibbs could do her business, and glanced at the basement entry through which the fire-setter had entered the house. Someone, probably a firefighter, had put a small piece of plywood over the broken pane.

The water truck had driven along this side of the house, and I stooped to examine one of the flattened bushes. The ground was soft enough for me to dig it up.

Something yellow caught my eye. A dog biscuit. And not the brand I bought. Mister Tibbs was immediately at my side to sniff it, so I held it out of reach. I stuck it in the pocket of my lightweight jacket. Surely no fingerprints on it, but I felt certain how the intruder had quieted Mister Tibbs.

Rain picked up as I stood. "Come on girl. You don't want to smell like wet dog." As we got close to the porch on the other side of the house, it began to pour. We ran quickly onto the covered porch.

"Sit, girl." Mister Tibbs obeyed, and I wiped her feet with a towel I'd placed by the door as we left. I gestured to Cat. "In you both go."

I carried the litter into the basement and sat it next to the litter box, which was suspiciously empty. I hoped Cat had a large bladder.

As I reached the top of the stairs, the house phone rang, and I grabbed it.

A hushed and garbled woman's voice said, "You stupid bitch. You told that reporter what to say!"

"Excuse me? Who is...?"

The woman had hung up. I glanced at the clock. The funeral and dinner had to be over. Had Janet Dodson called to tell me what she thought about the morning's article?

I pressed star and the number that redialed the last call, but the line was busy. I wished I had put caller ID on the phone when I hooked it back up.

Ambrose and I had paid a small fee to keep our parents' phone number assigned to us, but not on. Since I didn't plan to use the house phone much, I restarted the service with a basic plan with no options except voicemail.

"Nuts." I stared at the phone. It almost never rang. I'd have to try the redial again in a few minutes.

In the meantime, I took a plastic sandwich bag from a kitchen drawer, eased the dog biscuit into it without touching it further, and placed it on the counter. Now what?

I called the sheriff's office on my cell phone. Sophie told me he wasn't in the office, and I told her what I'd found near the side door. She said someone would get back to me.

I made a few calls using my cell phone to arrange to get Internet installed in the house. When the house phone rang, I grabbed it, wondering if it would be the same female caller.

"Melanie?"

"Hi, sheriff."

"Your cell phone went to voicemail. Sophie suggested your parents' old phone number."

"That's fine...oh, nuts!"

"Excuse me?"

"I had a call a few minutes ago and had tried to do auto-redial, but it was busy."

"No doubt they'll call again," he said, sounding irritated.

"Probably not." I relayed what the woman had said.

"Huh. Could mean something, could be a crank. I thought you called me about some bone in your yard."

"It's not what I buy for Mister Tibbs. I found it near the side door, when I walked Mister Tibbs a few minutes ago."

"Still have it?"

"Well, yeah. I put it in a plastic bag."

"If it's one of those larger, hard ones, maybe we can get a print."

"Sorry, it's one of the small, sort of crumbly ones."

Gallagher sighed. "Drop it off. You coming back into town today?"

"Hadn't planned on it, but I could."

"Tomorrow's okay. Might be useful for something, but not likely prints. Anything else?"

"Can you, uh, figure out who called me?"

He chuckled. "If it seems pertinent later, I can check with the county attorney to be sure we do it legally. For sure, let me know if you get any more calls."

"Will do. Thanks for returning my call."

After I hung up, I walked back to the kitchen. Cat sat on the counter. He looked over the edge to the floor, where he had pushed the plastic bag with the dog biscuit. Mister Tibbs sat licking her lips. She bent to sniff the now-empty plastic bag.

I yelled, "Get off the counter!"

Mister Tibbs assumed she was the target of the yell and scooted under the small kitchen table. Cat regarded me as if bored and jumped lightly to the floor, black tail swishing in annoyance.

I picked up the now-empty baggie. "Damn, damn, double damn!" I wished I hadn't called the sheriff.

A whine came from under the table.

I stooped and patted the floor next to me. Mister Tibbs emerged, tail and ears down. I scratched her head. "You don't want to do everything Cat suggests." She wagged her tail.

Irritated, I grabbed a tape measure to figure out the length of two living room walls. I wasn't sure if I wanted a couch or a loveseat, but figured price would dictate the choice.

As I measured, I considered next steps. I should be making follow-up calls, to see if potential clients were interested in hiring me for fall lawn cleanup or spring gardening.

Instead, I focused on how to figure out if Janet Dodson had clothes that smelled like smoke. It's a hard smell to be rid of.

Who would have thought a burn barrel would be so much trouble? But the town didn't collect garbage out in the county so… But Janet would have garbage. In fact, I thought Thursday was town garbage collection. A lot of people put their bags or cans at the curb the night before.

On TV shows like *Law and Order*, detectives always said trash at the curb was no longer private property. I didn't think I'd be arrested for taking a few black bags.

AT ELEVEN P.M. I PULLED onto the gravel road by my house. If I lived in Iowa City, no one would think twice about me leaving my house at this time of night. In farm country, with lights out at every farmhouse I passed, my truck could be noticed. I didn't turn my headlights on until I got into town.

To the extent River's Edge had a wealthy neighborhood, Janet Dodson lived in it. Her house was a split-level, one of only a few in town.

Two cars sat in the driveway. I realized she could have a lot of folks staying with her, so this might not be the time to snatch trash. On the other hand, if she had clothes or an empty can of fire starter, this would be the night to toss them out. House guests could mean more garbage to mix with incriminating stuff.

The only light inside the house was dim, maybe a night light. The back porch light was on, but not the front. And in front of the house sat two large, blue garbage bins, metal handles facing the street for a truck to pick them up without any human labor.

After the afternoon rain, the night was clear and cool. I drove past the house and around the block. I couldn't do that twice. A neighbor who slept lightly could hear the car and look out a window.

I parked at the edge of a large lot two doors down from the Dodson house. I left my pickup, but didn't lock it. I had no idea how many bags I could carry without being noticed, or how heavy the bags would be.

Fortunately, leaves in the street were damp, so they didn't crunch under my feet. The only street lamp was beyond the Dodson house, so I wouldn't be in a circle of light. My dinner of tuna casserole and broccoli roiled in my stomach.

Did I really want to do this? No, but how else would I learn anything?

The bins sat just past the edge of the driveway, and I skittered on some damp gravel. I swore softly and moved faster.

As I reached for the large lid on the closest bin, it occurred to me I should have on gloves. I pulled the sleeve of my fleece jacket over one hand, grasped the top handle, and swung it back. Two cardboard pizza boxes sat on top, and I gently sat them on the ground.

I lifted a black plastic sack from the bin, surprised by how light it was. I shook it gently. Sounded like a bunch of paper serving products. Maybe she'd had people over after the funeral and used disposable plates.

The next sack was so heavy I had a hard time lifting it from the bin. After promising myself I would take a hot bath when I got home, so my back didn't ache, I sat it on the ground and lifted the lighter bag and pizza boxes back into the can.

A soft whistle came through the night, followed by a man's low voice that said, "Come on boy."

I whispered, "Crud," as I lifted the bag to place it behind the bin. I walked fast, away from the sound of the voice. At the edge of Janet's yard, I ducked behind a hedge.

The voice came again. "We aren't out for a stroll. Do your business."

I couldn't see the dog, but heard its tags rattle. The man's voice sounded like Jody, who owned the hardware store. Andy's boss. He'd know I didn't live near here. I moved further into the darkness by the hedge.

"Don't sniff that bag!" Though the man's voice was hushed, the command was firm.

I could hear my heartbeat in my ears, and realized I had been holding my breath.

"Okay. Finally. Let's go back."

My heart slowed as Jody's footsteps grew faint. After a minute I stepped back into the street and moved quickly to the bins and the bag behind them. As I hefted the heavy bag, something dripped on my shoe. The dog had peed on the bag.

CHAPTER SIXTEEN

THE SIDE OF THE HOUSE that faced the cornfield couldn't be seen from the street, so I carried my bounty onto that porch. Mister Tibbs scratched on the interior door. If I was out, she was supposed to be, too.

I unlocked the door, and she bolted to the trash bag. Before I could stop her, she had smelled the other dog's urine and added hers.

I shut my eyes for a few seconds. "Go down the steps." She didn't have her leash, but I figured she was too interested in what I did to wander.

Cat meowed, and I grabbed the door handle to let him slink out. "This is getting ridiculous."

I leaned into the house and turned on the porch light. Then I had a smart idea and walked to the kitchen. I flicked on that light and grabbed a pitcher from under the sink. When I had filled it with warm water, I went back to the porch and poured it over the garbage bag.

Offended by splatter, Cat marched off the porch and sat next to Mister Tibbs, who peered up from the foot of the steps.

"Stay down there, you two."

Gingerly, I opened the draw string and peered in. Most of the contents appeared to be kitchen trash, though the middle of the bag had a stack of Tom Dodson's funeral programs. "Huh. You'd think she'd keep these. Maybe they printed a lot of extras."

I hadn't yet read the material that I'd stuck in my purse, so I sat on one of the two camp chairs and opened the program. Dodson's life was summed up in three paragraphs, and was similar to many in South County. Born here, he *proudly chose to remain in Southeast Iowa and, with his wife Janet, raise their daughter.*

The last two sentences were odd. "Tom was known for his friendliness and periodic donations to local charities. He also was not afraid to say when he made a mistake."

"Weird." I supposed a lot of people wouldn't admit when they were wrong. Or was Janet passively chastising him for some transgression? And 'periodic?' That sounded like he only donated when forced to.

I tossed the program onto the porch floor and went back to the bag. Heavier items had fallen to the bottom, and most were men's toiletries. I figured Janet was clearing out Tom's partially used bathroom items, until I saw unopened bottles of shampoo and conditioner, in gray bottles typical of men's products, and shaving cream. "She really didn't want any reminders."

Finally, a woodsy smell reached me. I pulled out a dark flannel shirt that reeked of smoke. "Stinky." I looked at the tag – men's large. *Good use for her late husband's shirt.*

My elation began to dissipate. I needed more than a smelly shirt to prove Janet Dodson broke into my house and burned those files. And drugged Mister Tibbs.

I wished I'd bought external security cameras last spring. Too expensive, except in retrospect when the pictures would come in handy.

I wondered if Janet had kept any of my dad's files. The thought hadn't crossed my mind previously. Maybe she took them home to read and then tossed them. But not in this bag.

I'd been so anxious to leave with the one bag, I hadn't opened the second blue bin. Did I have the guts to go back there? Surely no one would be walking dogs at one a.m.

For almost a minute I considered this option, then slowly shook my head. I couldn't possibly be lucky twice tonight. Not just in finding something useful, but in doing so without being seen.

Besides, wouldn't it make more sense to throw out work-related files at the grain elevator? I didn't see me dumpster diving. "It would be worth it to find some of Dad's files." I'd have to think about it.

Meantime, what would I do with the damn shirt? I remembered a lecture the sheriff had given me after Hal Morris was killed. It did little good for me to find evidence. How did anyone know I hadn't put the object where I located it? "You should have told Gallagher your idea. Then he could have found it."

Except he would likely have poo-poo'd the notion and not looked.

I sat with the shirt in my hand for several seconds, thinking. I would keep it. Maybe I'd be the one to confront Janet Dodson with burning those files, and the shirt would be my evidence. "Evidence. Listen to yourself."

Frustrated, I looked toward the bottom of the porch steps. No animals, and I didn't see them. I whistled and was rewarded with rustling from the dried corn stalks. Mister Tibbs dashed out and ran to me. She gave the smoke-smelling shirt a good sniff.

Cat was a few seconds behind her, but I realized he was chasing something. He pounced, stood with a field mouse in his teeth and shook it hard. The farmer in me knew a fast kill was kinder than a slow one, but I always hated to see it.

I opened the door, and Mister Tibbs ran into the house. Cat walked toward me. "Uh uh. Eat it out here, and then you can come in."

He padded up the steps and dropped the mouse at my feet.

I WOKE THURSDAY MORNING feeling impatient. I needed to focus more on my landscaping business and less on whoever broke into the house. The person got what they wanted. How likely was it they would come again?

I made a mental note to get window alarms of some sort. If Jody couldn't order them for me, I'd drive to Fairfield or Ottumwa.

After I fed Cat and Mister Tibbs and walked her, I showered and sat at my kitchen table making a list of what to do during the day. Fortunately, it would be in the fifties, so I had a good day to work outside if I needed to.

- Make calls to businesses that got flyers.
- Get grass seed for here and Syl's.
- Spread it
- Furniture
- Estimates from elevators
- Farm Bureau

I was kidding myself to think I'd get all that done. I wanted to check out Dodson Grain Elevator. They had to have a dumpster. And maybe a staff member who would talk to me about grain elevator finances. But that would be a stretch. I knew a few of the employees by sight, but no one personally.

To ensure I got something constructive done, I grabbed the county phone book and called some of the businesses where I'd left flyers. The antique store said they really couldn't afford it. My mom had really liked its owner, so I offered to put a smaller pot by their front door in the spring. For free. I hung up quickly, when it sounded as if Mrs. Moffitt was going to cry.

The Farm Bureau was housed in its insurance office. Tom Dodson had been vice-president. What could they tell me?

"No, you're supposed to be thinking about your own work."

Mister Tibbs grunted from her spot at my feet, apparently endorsing the idea.

I'd left a flyer with Andy to give to Jody at the hardware and implement store. I doubted it made it to Jody's desk, but I called anyway.

"Melanie. Haven't seen you in a while."

"I was in the other day to get doorknobs to replace some here at the house."

"Good, good."

After a two second pause, I asked, "I figured if you wanted a pot of flowers in front of your store you would plant them, but I thought I'd call. This time of year, I'd just be putting in cabbage plants and a few pansies."

"Hmm. I saw your flyer. It didn't mention price."

"Not expensive. Twenty-five dollars in the spring and again in the fall, but you have to water them." I wanted to say it would give Andy something to do, but refrained.

"You supply the pot?"

"I do. I talked to Andy in the spring about checking on some larger sizes, but I guess it didn't work out. I go over to Keosauqua to get them."

I could envision smoke coming out of Jody's ears during the five seconds when he said nothing.

"Gee, Melanie. I'm not sure how that fell through the cracks. How about I give you the one for here, and you buy some of the others from us?"

I walked into that. He didn't quote a price, but I didn't see how it could be higher than what I'd paid, and I wouldn't have to drive fifteen miles. We talked for a minute about ceramic versus heavy plastic, and then hung up.

I looked under the table. "One more customer."

Mister Tibbs opened her eyes halfway and thumped her tail once.

I didn't have any other takers, but one was better than none. I trekked to the barn, to get two of the bags of topsoil I had stored there, and left for town.

WHEN I GOT TO FARM AND MORE, a sullen Andy greeted me. "Sorry about the pots, Mel. Guess I forgot."

I shrugged. "I figured it didn't work out. I brought some topsoil so I can plant a pot today, if Jody has one ready."

"I'll bring it out." Andy loped toward the back of the store.

I headed to the lawn and garden section, which now had mostly fertilizer, pumpkins, and lawn ornaments, and picked out some grass seed. I planned to seed near the house. We drove on the land between the house and barn when we needed to, so the dirt was hard. Plus, I didn't want a lot to mow.

Andy came back with a large brown, heavy-duty plastic pot. Ugly. Jody had said he would order several in bright colors for me to use around town.

After a short debate with Andy, we decided to place the pot a few feet to the left of the entry door. Left as you faced the store. On the other side Jody had a batch of snow throwers chained together. In the spring the space held lawnmowers.

I dumped two bags of topsoil in the pot and added two cabbage and four multi-colored pansy plants.

Andy came back out to stare at the results. "Looks kind of bare."

"The decorative cabbage plants really spread out. The pansies will a bit, too."

He nodded. "Kinda weird to put in plants in October."

"These'll last a while. Especially so close to the building."

When he said nothing else, I collected the empty soil bags and placed them and my trowel in the back of the pickup. The grain elevator beckoned.

THE SIGN ANNOUNCING TOM'S death no longer stood in front of the Dodson Grain Elevator office. I thought it odd to be down so quickly, but maybe Janet didn't want everyone mentioning it when they came in.

I had parked at the far edge of the small lot, hoping to be able to see behind the office. I couldn't, but I hadn't needed to. A brown dumpster, much smaller than I expected, sat to the right of the building.

I opened the door to see a friendly face behind the counter, and grinned. "Sam!"

"Hey, Melanie, good to see you."

Sam and I sat together to sell our produce at the summer farmers' markets. "Didn't know you worked here." A quick glance around the space told me he kept it cleaner than I remembered. A potted plant on a table near the window made me think maybe Janet was responsible.

"Just part-time. Started at the end of the summer."

Every farmer I knew, except older ones like the Donovans, had a second job of some sort. Unless, like Ambrose, their spouse's job got them health insurance. He lived to farm.

"So, you probably heard Ambrose and I will be able to farm our land again next summer."

His nod was somber. "I was sorry about Old Man Frost, but I'm glad you can live there again."

"Me, too." I leaned on the counter. "Listen, I'll have to get some volume info from the Kendigs, since we rented to them. But in the meantime, I thought I could get some basic price info from you, for next year."

"Sure." Sam reached beneath the counter for some material.

Janet Dodson's voice came from an enclosed office behind the front space. "Melanie. What a surprise."

I had not expected to see her, but why should she sit home all day? "Janet. I hope yesterday went as well as it could."

"I didn't see you." Her look, and arched eyebrows, could best be described as chilly. It matched her outfit of a royal blue pants suit and silver top. Not what you usually see in an agricultural business.

Sam had frozen, and I almost stuttered. "I thought it might be hard for you to see me at the funeral. I stopped by to sign the book in the morning."

Her expression didn't exactly warm, but her shoulders seemed to relax. "Thoughtful of you. I had a lot of friends there."

I nodded, unsure what else to say.

Sam had regained movement and placed the paperwork on the counter in front of him.

Janet glanced at it. "Bringing your business to us?"

"I promised Ambrose I'd get both estimates, but I can't see driving grain out to Hopewell's." *As if I'd tell her no.*

She turned to Sam. "I'm heading over to the bank to switch all the accounts to my name. Be back in an hour or so."

Sam flushed. "Yes, ma'am."

Janet went back to the interior office, and I heard her leave by a side door. I met Sam's gaze. "Tough time to work here, I guess."

"She's had a rough couple days. I went to the funeral. She was a real trooper."

I nodded. "I hate funerals."

"Me, too." Sam went over basic costs per ton of grain and put a couple of brochures in an envelope for me.

I gestured around the room. "Looks nice. Did you guys paint?"

"Yep. And Tom did some reorganizing. We cleared out the supply room in the back and put some of the stuff in the attic. He put a couch and TV in there."

"Guess he worked long hours." *And maybe used the couch for trysts?*

Sam nodded. "I don't know if Janet will do that. Maybe she'll hire a manager or something."

I pretended to search for words and lowered my voice. "Sandi said there was a collection for the funeral, but I wasn't sure who was handling the money."

He smiled broadly. "Good news there. Janet didn't initially know the combination of the office safe. When she opened it there was…" He looked stricken, probably thinking he shouldn't be talking about company finances.

I smiled. "No worries. I'm glad for her." *And maybe we know where Tom Dodson hid some of the money he embezzled.*

CHAPTER SEVENTEEN

AT THE FARM BUREAU INSURANCE office, I was unpleasantly surprised to see Ryan. We seemed to make a mutual decision to act friendly in front of Victor, the agent, whose last name I couldn't remember.

"Hey Mel," Victor said.

I smiled. "Back at you, Victor. If you're busy I can come back later."

Victor is in his late forties and has a perpetually nervous demeanor. "Ryan and I were just chatting." He focused on Ryan. "Did you get what you need?"

Ryan shrugged. "Not much to get." He looked at me. "You can guess the story I'm covering."

I nodded, but looked at Victor. "I'm sorry you guys lost Tom."

"And I'm sorry you had the experience of finding him," Victor said.

"Me, too. So, I thought I'd get some figures on crop insurance, since Ambrose and I will be farming our land again."

Victor nodded his bald head vigorously. "Since you two didn't personally handle it earlier, I'll give you the packet for new customers." He walked into a small office behind the reception desk.

Ryan stood stiffly. "Sheriff's office is pretty tight on this one."

I nodded, trying not to show the irritation I felt about his Wednesday article. "All I've heard is it was a blow to the back of the head."

He lowered his voice. "And no suspects at all, from what I've heard."

Victor returned with a fancy folder that had a gleaming photo of a green field of corn and bright red barn. "So, Melanie, let's go over a few things, then you and Ambrose can read more at home and call to set up an appointment."

Ryan said goodbye and left.

I had the sense Victor wasn't anxious to talk to me, and his conversation seemed terse.

"Did I do something to offend you, Victor?"

He flushed. "No, not at all. Sheriff Gallagher, uh, he said..."

I laughed to cover my annoyance. "I'm not here to pump you. I just hope they find the killer soon, so people can relax about it. Especially Janet Dodson."

His head bobbed. "Yes, especially Janet."

I shook my head. "It's the reporter in me, but I can't figure out why anyone would go after him in a church basement."

He sighed. "No one can. Personally, I think someone saw all the cars and came in to see what was going on."

"And he surprised them, you think?"

He shrugged. "Could be. Maybe it was someone who wasn't supposed to be there, and they thought Tom would cause them trouble. Don't think he had enemies."

I left, thinking I'd wasted my time.

Ryan leaned against my truck. "Truce?"

"I doubt I know anything you don't."

He smiled. "You know what we always say. Maybe you don't know what you know."

I regarded his lanky frame. As the paper's intern, his hair had been longer. After Hal died, Doc Shelton told him it was unprofessional, so he had it cut. He now seemed older than twenty-one.

"Any news on Hal's successor?"

He shook his head. "Doc and the others are pretty tight-lipped. I don't think they like the pool of applicants."

"And Sandi says Scott won't stay."

"He might, but his wife won't. He said she misses her friends."

Scott and his wife were black, and as friendly as River's Edge was, each census showed that South County still had roughly two-hundred black people. Of course, the total River's Edge population was only about 7,000. Still, Iowa City was a lot more diverse.

"I have to get going, Ryan."

He moved a foot or so from my truck. "Do you really think the burn barrel fire and Tom's murder are unrelated?"

I stared at him, and he dropped his gaze. "I think it's an odd coincidence. I had picked up the files from Mrs. Keyser's house, but I was home. Who would be dumb enough to risk breaking in, if they could be linked to the murder?"

He shrugged. "Depends on what they thought was in the files."

"Gotta go, Ryan."

"See you." He walked toward the red Fiesta.

As I pulled away from the Farm Bureau office, I remembered my earlier assumption that, for Tom to embezzle money, he had to have someone in accounting working with him. I could stop by the library to talk to Ginny Forman.

I'd have to find a way to ask how broad her duties had been at the grain elevator. That could be tricky. It's not as if I could ask if she helped Tom Dodson overstate expenses so he could hide money.

The small library parking lot had only Ginny's Camry. I left my windows cracked to let in the cool fall air and walked to the door.

Town budget restrictions meant hours had been cut back. Lucky for me, the sign said **Open**. The door tinkled as I entered, and I searched for Ginny.

Her voice called from shelves at the far end of the library. "Be right with you." She either had a cold or had been crying.

I responded with, "No rush." I'm not a big crier. When I'm especially sad I tend to go quiet. I could certainly understand grieving about someone you worked with every day. Except maybe Hal.

In less than a minute Ginny came toward where I stood at the circulation desk. Her expensive looking navy-blue sweater and slacks were more formal than clothes other librarians wore.

"Hi, Ginny. I thought I'd stop by. Seems like a writer and a librarian should know each other better."

"Oh, do you freelance now?"

"My lawn and garden business keeps me busy, but I wouldn't mind doing some after I settle into a routine. What are you up to?"

She pointed to a stack of books on the counter, as she walked behind it. "I'm staying busy by sorting some of the recent book donations."

"Ah. For the annual sale?"

She nodded. "It's a lot of work, but we get most of our money for new books from it. You know how tight the town budget always is."

"I hear you. How do you like such a people job?" When she looked puzzled, I added, "I mean, I guess accounting could be kind of solitary."

She shrugged. "Sometimes. I did the billing, so customers called a fair bit."

I gave her what I hoped was a genuine-looking smile. "Bet it's more fun here. I ran into Sam this morning when I stopped by to get info on a contract for next year. Did he take your place?"

She stiffened. "He does some of the customer calls and such, but Janet Dodson decided she wanted to be more involved in the business."

I grimaced. "She was there today. As you might figure, I'm not her favorite person."

She frowned. "Not her…oh. It's not your fault you, um found him."

"Sorry, I shouldn't bring it up. I stopped by to say hello, and here I am bringing up unpleasant topics."

She reached under the counter to get a tissue. "I didn't really know Tom all that well, but it's still hard to think that someone you worked with was murdered."

I pretended to be flustered. "I should let you go. I hope your day gets easier."

"Thanks."

Back in my truck I leaned my head against the seat. Did Janet Dodson want to "be more involved in the business" because she figured it should be generating more income for their household? Or did she suspect her husband was having a fling? If she did, did she think of Ginny or simply want to be sure no attractive woman spent time with him all day?

Or maybe Janet was bored at home. Whatever the motivation, it sounded as if she had forced Ginny out. But even though I believed Janet burned my dad's files, she didn't kill Tom, so where did that leave me?

AS I ATE A GRILLED CHEESE sandwich in Mason's Diner, I asked myself whether I was more interested in who drugged Mister Tibbs and set the burn barrel fire, or who killed Tom Dodson. The answer was Mister Tibbs. But unlike what I'd implied to Ryan, I did think the two events overlapped.

I saw no clear path to get more information on Dodson's death. The sheriff wouldn't share, and most homicides were personal. I knew little about Dodson's life. I believed he had skimmed money from his company, and instinct told me he'd spent at least some of it on a girlfriend.

Was that woman Brenda Chase or Ginny Forman? Maybe. But had there been others before or after them? I saw Janet Dodson as cold, but maybe she had become that way because of her husband's behavior. *A couch in the back room. Could he have been more obvious?*

If Janet had not been with people the entire time her husband was out of the community room, I'd at least speculate that she killed him. But why do it at the Farm Bureau dinner? She had plenty of private time to do away with him.

Sandi slid into the booth across from me. "What are you up to, Mel?"

I studied her, not smiling. "I'm beginning to wonder if you have a deal with Shirley to tip you off whenever I come into the diner."

"She couldn't pay me enough, Shug." Shirley grinned as if proud she'd overheard my comment.

I smiled. "I don't know, Shirley. Maybe you could save enough to buy the diner for yourself."

She almost snorted. "No way." She took out her order pad. "I need you both for my sources."

Sandi raised her eyebrows at me. "I think Mel must not have slept well."

Shirley addressed Sandi. "What'll it be?"

"I'll take the chili, with lots of crackers."

"Anything else, Melanie?" Shirley asked.

"I'm good." As Shirley walked away, I lowered my voice to Sandi. "No date tonight?"

"Funny. What's eating you?"

"Just tired of not knowing who drugged Mister Tibbs."

Sandi slipped out of her jacket. "You know, if you still worked for the paper you'd have more of a reason to ask around."

"Are you asking?"

"I'm listening, but I didn't think you wanted the bit about Mister Tibbs blabbed all over town."

I sighed. "You're right. I'm half-annoyed because I ran into Ryan at the Farm Bureau insurance office. He's trying to get me to say I think Tom's murder and my fire are related."

She narrowed her eyes. "Don't you think they are?"

I picked up my sandwich again. "Thanks to Mrs. Keyser and her mouth, they could be. But I don't want him drawing the parallel in the paper."

Sandi looked away and back again. "Heard about the autopsy."

I did a gimme gesture with the hand not holding my grilled cheese.

"Blow to the head, and it seems he broke a couple fingers on one hand, likely because he fell on them."

"Hmm. He grabbed my shirt, but I don't think I noted his other hand."

"The odd thing is, the indentation on his head is kind of like a half moon shape. What do you suppose would do that?"

My mind envisioned the cleaning supply room. "I guess half of something round."

Sandi nodded. "And Ryan's mother's cousin said they can't figure out what it was."

"Deputy Bob…I can't remember his last name," I murmured.

"I think it's Rogers, but I don't talk to him much. What would be in easy reach in a church basement coat closet?"

"I usually keep my coat with me in church, so I don't go into that closet. You know, I've seen an umbrella stand in there."

Sandi shrugged. "Kind of big to raise above someone's head and hit with that much force."

I didn't mention St. Francis. I sat up straighter. "Sometimes there's a box to collect canned goods down there. I don't know about in the closet."

Shirley plopped chili in front of Sandi and ceremoniously took five or six packs of crackers from her apron pocket and slid them onto the table. "Cans for what? The food pantry?"

"Yes," I said. "Do you guys have any extra stuff? I guess it could be dented cans, as long as they haven't been around forever."

Shirley frowned. "I know you're thinking about a murder weapon." She turned on her heel and made for the kitchen.

I shrugged. "I guess I insulted her."

Sandi opened two packs of crackers and added them to her chili. "She'll get over it next time she wants to know something."

"The edges of cans are pretty thin. Did the autopsy report say how thick the half-moon indent was?"

She took a bite of chili, and I could see her mentally going over the report. "I don't think I saw it put that way. The report mentioned the depth of the injury. More than a quarter-inch."

"Sounds like he was hit hard. You have the report?"

Sandi shook her head. "Scott has it, and he didn't want us making copies."

"Gallagher probably gave him a copy on condition he didn't share it."

"I think it was the ME. Scott's kind of buddied up to Dr. MacGregor."

"Ah. Makes more sense."

Sandi opened more crackers. "So, Mel, I heard a rumor that Doc Shelton might ask you to be editor."

I ate my last potato chip. "I like my business."

"You could keep it. I think the advisory group believes the paper should cut back to two issues per week."

My eyebrows went up. "Why?"

"Less advertising revenue."

"But a new editor will pound the pavement for more ads. And people will be more willing to buy from a new person than from Hal."

Sandi grinned. "So when they offer the job to you, make sure to bargain for three days for at least a couple of months."

CHAPTER EIGHTEEN

WHEN I READ RYAN'S FRIDAY article, I was glad I had the paper delivered at the farm again. I nearly blew a gasket, and that could have gotten me kicked out of the diner.

Ryan's heading was **Farm Owner Thinks Fire and Murder an Odd Coincidence**.

I mentally went over my conversation with Ryan outside the Farm Bureau insurance office. I had used those words, but he had deliberately taken them out of context. I had followed that statement by saying since I was home, it didn't make sense that someone would be dumb enough to risk breaking in after they just committed murder. Or something to that effect.

Right after the statement mentioning I thought the two events coincided somehow, he said that my father's files were in the boxes burned and that my dad and others thought Tom charged "more than necessary" to process and store grain.

More than angry, I was embarrassed. The article made it seem as if I had given Ryan the information and thought I knew more than the sheriff. I came off sounding like an attention-seeker. *Gallagher's going to give me an earful.*

I called Ryan's cell phone. When he picked up, I said, "You're a real jerk," and hung up. I didn't answer when he called back.

FRIDAY AFTERNOON, I WATCHED Mister Tibbs' eyes roam through Syl's property. She didn't like sharing the space with Cat. She sat within two feet of me and watched Cat's every move.

My curly-haired pup only stirred if Cat left her line of sight and she deemed it necessary to follow him.

I glanced down as Mister Tibbs crept toward the barn, a generous term for the dark red building that was big enough for only a couple of genteel horses. Or, in Syl's case, a riding mower, wheelbarrow, and assorted lawn tools.

I called after Mister Tibbs. "He'll be back. He knows who feeds him." Mister Tibbs ignored me and continued to slink after Cat.

My pets and I had come to Syl's on a sunny Friday to take advantage of the fifty-degree weather. Stooper was happily working on a headstone for Tom Dodson, per a phone call he received yesterday evening from Janet.

I raked leaves behind the house for perhaps twenty minutes, then stooped to scoop a pile of leaves into the recycling bag that I would dump in Syl's burn barrel. I again wished he'd let Stooper and me create a stone-encircled fire ring behind the barn. I could wait to light the fire until it was piled high with leaves and brush. The burn barrel constantly went out because a single bag of dry leaves burned so fast.

Because a pile of branches, the product of mid-October wind gusts, waited to be burned, I began to cut those into smaller lengths. Most were thin enough for heavy-duty clippers, but a couple put my gas chain saw into action.

Cat had not heard the noisy saw before, and Mister Tibbs hated it. When my shoulders tired and I placed it on the ground for a couple of minutes, I glanced toward the barn. My two pets sat almost shoulder-to-shoulder by the sliding barn door. Apparently, they had found a mutual enemy in the chain saw.

I whittled the pile of dry wood into a neat stack of short limbs and had taken a second break, when a voice startled me.

"You're pretty good with a saw."

I turned so fast I stumbled, but regained my balance. *Thank God I wasn't holding the chain saw.* "Janet. What are you doing out here?"

The more pertinent question was why she held a hunting rifle at her right side. It looked incongruous next to her dark green skirt, white turtleneck, and chunky gold necklace. "I don't think Syl lets anyone hunt on his property."

She trilled a high-pitched laugh. "His puny little farmette. I'm not hunting deer."

I kept my voice steady. "Then you can put your rifle back in your..." I glanced at the long driveway. "SUV."

She had parked it near the street. Between the saw and the car's distance from me, I hadn't noticed her arrival.

"You're the only person who thought Tom took money off the top. You should have stopped talking about it."

The fall breeze decided to pick up, and a batch of leaves swirled at my feet. "I don't know he did that, but my father and some others wondered about it a few years ago."

She raised the rifle in a dismissive gesture. "Tom just wanted to talk to your father."

The pit of my stomach turned cold. "When was that?"

"You know the night. Tom wanted to stop him before he got to that dinner. Arnold Perkins was going to convince a bunch of people to get Tom to sell. Tell 'em Tom...*hiccup*...charged too much."

"So...what? He followed my parents' car? Why would Tom want to kill them over money from your own business?"

"He didn't want to kill them. He wanted them to pull over, you know, on the...*hiccup*...shoulder." She swayed slightly.

The cold feeling in the pit of my stomach moved up to my chest. I mentally measured the distance between us. About fifteen feet. She seemed pretty drunk. Would I have time to tackle her from the front before she could get off a shot?

Something in my posture alerted Janet, and she pointed the rifle toward me, still not held high enough to shoot. "Stay over there!"

I raised my hands in mock surrender and dropped them again. "I like it over here. Would you, uh, like to have a seat? The barn has a couple of lawn chairs in it." Not really, but it could get her moving, which I saw as good for me.

She grinned so broadly her lips thinned across her upper gums. "I'm not staying long."

"Can't say I'll be sorry to see you go." I gestured toward the chain saw at my feet. "So, I have a lot of work to do. You could…"

"Eww." Janet gaped at Cat, who was rubbing his head against her leg. "You'll ruin my stockings. Go away!"

Mister Tibbs sat about ten feet from Cat, closer to the barn. I didn't want Janet shooting at either animal. "Scat you two!"

Cat had apparently tired of his head rub and wandered away. Mister Tibbs sat still, except to move her head between the two human speakers.

If Janet hadn't seemed so drunk I might have thought she was making up the information about my parents. At this point, I doubted she could fabricate a cogent lie.

I kept my eyes on her rifle. "I don't think something I said or did had anything to do with Tom's death. Besides…"

Should I say this? Why not? Because she has a gun. I said it anyway. "You saw my dad's files before you burned them. Nothing there to hurt Tom."

She actually giggled, then swayed so far to one side that, if I'd been closer, I could have ducked and grabbed the rifle barrel from below.

"Shows what chu…you know."

That statement sounded like an admission that the financial reports showed that costs were inflated to help the Dodsons embezzle funds. But it wasn't quite an admission that she was the one who burned the files.

"I only wish I'd figured out that slut killed him." Janet swayed slightly. "The sheriff said you didn't do it, but I honest to God thought you did."

"Slut? Janet, who are you talking about?"

"You know. That pretty little librarian. She was the reason he wanted that cash I didn't know about."

"Uh, was Ginny extorting money?"

"Don't say her name!" Janet blew out a breath in a whoosh. "No! Sleeping with the devious bastard. He was her sugar daddy. But he stopped after he decided to come back to me."

That explained the twenty-five thousand dollar car. Just good enough to be a nice gift, not so gaudy that people would wonder how a small-town librarian could afford it.

"Uh, how can you be sure she killed him?"

Janet tossed her head as if poo-pooing my question. Then she cackled like the wicked witch in *The Wizard of Oz*. "I have my ways, my pretty."

She must be truly insane.

"If Ginny ended up with some of the money, money that should be yours, maybe you can sue her. Or something."

"Oh, I took care of her. Almost, anyway."

The cold feeling in my stomach returned. "What did you do, Janet?"

She burped. "Excuse me. You don't need to know. Nobody needs to know." She giggled. "She won't need any more money."

If I could get the rifle away from her, I could call the sheriff. Get him to search for Ginny. Given Janet's condition, maybe her words were just that. Ginny could be arranging books on library shelves.

Janet tilted her head. "You're swaying! Stop it!"

"I think that's you. How about we find those chairs?"

"Shut up!"

Janet clearly wasn't used to drinking. If she aimed a rifle as well as she held her liquor, I might get out of this as a breathing person. And maybe help find Ginny Forman, wherever she was. If she was still alive.

I glanced toward the back of Syl's house, wishing he would come home. "Look, Janet, at this point all you've done is come up to me with that old rifle. That's not such a bad…"

"New…*hiccup*…to me. Bought it with some of my dear, departed husband's slush fund."

"I'm sorry he," I searched for the right word, "betrayed you. I wish I could make it right for you." *And I hope you don't make it a lot worse by killing me.*

"You know what's the bad part?"

"Uh, not really."

"He dumped her and said he wanted to spend our golden years together." She started to sob, but stopped herself. "If he'd died a few months ago, I wouldn't miss the bastard at all."

"I sometimes wish I could turn back the clock." *Like convince my father not to drive that night.*

"I don't give a damn about a clock." Her eyes filled with tears. "All I'm doing now is protecting my husband's memory."

"And your business, I think. It's all your money now, Janet."

I had made a huge error.

"It's not about the money!" Her face reddened in an instant, and she raised the rifle to her shoulder faster than I thought she could. I ducked, but she lowered the barrel, still aiming at my head.

Something long and black streaked across my line of vision. Cat jumped up and dug her claws into Janet's chest, which forced her to drop the rifle and raise her hands toward Cat's neck.

Mister Tibbs and I reached her before she could choke our cat.

AARON GRANGER IS MY least favorite deputy sheriff, but when his car flew into Syl's driveway after my 9-1-1 call, I would have offered him the profit from next year's corn crop.

He ran toward where Janet lay sobbing on the ground, my dirty work boot on her back and Cat and Mister Tibbs by her head.

"What the hell, Melanie?" He reached us and stared down at Janet.

"She, she attached me," Janet said, fury evident in her gulping sobs.

I shifted my gaze from Granger to her. "I think you mean attacked. Which I most definitely didn't."

"My clothes are ruined! Let me up."

I nodded toward the ground a few feet from Janet. "That's her rifle. She's mad at me for figuring out Tom cooked his books."

"He never cooked! I had to do all the cooking!" She sobbed, then spit out some dirt.

Granger, who stands just more than six feet tall with straight posture and broad shoulders, used a foot to move the rifle even further beyond Janet's reach. Then he regarded my boot. "You can let her up."

I took my foot off her spine and massaged my calf, which was sore from applying constant pressure to her back.

"Listen here, Janet," Granger barked. "I'm going to haul you up and cuff you. I don't want you fighting me. I'd have to Taser you."

He ignored my glance at his belt, which bore no Taser.

Face in the dirt, Janet said, "You should cuff that bitch."

I paused the massage. "Stop insulting my dog."

Granger almost smiled, but Janet didn't move from the ground. He asked, "Janet, did Syl Seaton invite you out here today?"

She said nothing.

In the excitement of having the rifle aimed at me and watching my animals team up on her, I'd forgotten Janet's ominous remarks about Ginny. "I think she might have Ginny Forman locked up somewhere."

Granger bent over and hoisted Janet to her feet. She kind of backed into him. He pushed her away with one arm, as he unclipped cuffs from his belt with the other, then drew her right hand behind her back. "You're on private property, wielding a weapon. We're going to visit with the sheriff for a while."

Her voice rose to a screech. "What are you doing? Who do you think you are?" She swayed and tried to turn to face him, but couldn't.

With her right hand in its cuff, he reached for her left and pulled it behind her. "I'm Deputy Sheriff Aaron Granger, and you're going to tell me where to find Ginny Forman."

CHAPTER NINETEEN

SYL SAT WITH ME AT the table in Gallagher's office. Since the melee had taken place on his property, Gallagher had called him as Syl drove back into town.

But I would have called Syl if Gallagher hadn't. Ambrose lived three hours away, and after hearing what Janet said about my parents' deaths, I wanted a friend's reassuring presence as I gave a statement.

From down the hall, Janet continued her protests. Some of the booze had worn off, and her anger sounded more rational. "Her cat and dog pushed me to the damn ground!"

Gallagher's voice reached us, but I couldn't discern his words.

Syl's eyebrows went up. "Really?"

I nodded. "She had just raised the rifle toward me. I think if she'd done it more slowly, Cat wouldn't have reacted. He went for her throat."

"Guess it's a good thing you didn't leave him on the street outside Patel's place. You really owe that rascal a name."

My cell phone chirped, and I glanced at it. "Sandi." I hesitated.

"I didn't hear Gallagher tell you no calls."

I grinned at Syl. "I can blame you if he gets irritated." I answered the call. "Sandi."

"What the hell, Mel? Ambrose just called me to see if I knew what was up."

"Huh. Wonder why he didn't call me?"

Sandi shouted, "That's not the point!"

"Who told him?"

"How would I know? Where are you? I drove to Syl's. I saw a sheriff's car, but not your truck."

"I'm in Gallagher's office. I'm fine. Thanks to Ryan's article, Janet thought I had accused Tom of embezzlement."

"And…?"

"So, she uh, went to Syl's to find me. With a rifle."

Syl's tone held controlled laughter. "Tell her about the rascal who saved you."

"Why is Syl with you?"

He did a gimme gesture with one hand, so I gave him the phone.

"Because it was my property, so Gallagher had someone call me. I don't think Mel knows any more. She'll call Ambrose." He pressed off and handed me the phone.

I opened and shut my mouth. "She'll be mad for a week." I dialed Ambrose's number.

He answered before I'd heard a ring. "Mel, what the hell?"

"Do you know how many people have said that to me in the last week?"

"Are you okay? Why didn't you answer my calls?"

"I guess the equipment and stuff in this building interfered, and…"

"What building?"

"Sorry, I'm sitting in the sheriff's office. With Syl. But I'm not in trouble or anything."

"I told you to leave that stuff alone," Ambrose said.

I kept my tone cool. "It's been a while since I've needed someone to tell me what to do."

Syl's amused expression was replaced by a somber one, and Ambrose said, more quietly, "I know that. I meant it seemed like the Dodsons had been up to no good. And when there's money involved, people can get madder than a randy goat."

I recounted the thirty-second summary of events. I debated whether to tell Ambrose what Janet had said about Tom looking for

Mom and Dad the night they died. It didn't seem right to wait. "There's more."

Hot tears started down my cheeks, and Syl reached for my hand and laid his over it on the table.

I sniffed. "Janet pretty much said Tom Dodson wanted to run Mom and Dad off the road that... You know, the night of the accident." I took my hand from under Syl's and dug a wrinkled tissue from the pocket of my jeans.

Syl's furrowed brow deepened from concern to anger, but he said nothing. He stood and retrieved a box of tissues from Gallagher's desk and returned to the table.

Ambrose finally said something. "Why did she think that? And did she say he did?"

I blew my nose. "Dodson seemed to think Dad would mention the elevator finances to some people at the potluck they were driving to. Janet said he 'just wanted to talk' to them, but I had the clear impression his car directed Mom and Dad's to veer into that truck."

I sobbed hard, and Syl pulled me to him in a hug. Or as much as two people can hug when they're sitting next to each other in hard chairs.

Gallagher's harsh voice came from the door to his office. "What in blazes do you mean?"

We pulled apart, and I looked at my phone. Ambrose was still connected. I pushed the speaker button and turned to Gallagher. "Janet said Tom Dodson wanted to get Dad to pull onto the shoulder. To talk to him. That night."

Gallagher glanced at the phone. "Ambrose?"

He and I both said, "Yes."

Gallagher took a thin notebook from his breast pocket. "I've been interviewing her about today and the files that got burned at your place. I'm going back. But," he glanced at me, "Janet's been pretty drunk. Doesn't mean she lied about Tom going after your parents that night."

Going after?

"But," he continued, "she could have mixed up a bunch of different events. I'll speak to her some tonight, more tomorrow when I'm sure she's not on anything."

I stared at Gallagher. "But you'll keep her here, right?"

He nodded. "If she starts acting suicidal or something, I'll have to take her to the locked unit at the hospital, maybe transfer her someplace else. But I've got enough to hang onto her. I gotta get back to it." He walked out of the room, toward the area where Janet had been shouting a short time ago.

I called after him. "What about Ginny?"

Janet's voice came from down the hall. "That bitch!"

Gallagher's voice rose to a roar. "Be quiet, Janet!" He came back to the doorway. "I got three guys searching for her. You have any ideas?"

I shrugged. "I don't know her well enough to say anything besides the library. She drives a gold-colored Camry."

"We know that." He left again.

"Ginny who works at the elevator?" Ambrose asked.

"She's been the children's librarian for maybe a year. Apparently, she had an affair with Dodson."

Ambrose swore, and Syl whistled.

Ambrose shouted, "Get the hell away from those curtains! Oh, damn!"

Syl sat up straighter. "What!?"

I almost smiled. "Probably his goats." I raised my voice so Ambrose could hear me. "What did they do?"

Ambrose's voice came from a few feet away from his phone. "Wait a sec." A sharp thud on his end made me think he'd shut a window.

He came back to the phone. "I had the window that's over the porch open. No screen, but no bugs this time of year. One of the little bastards took two huge bites from her curtains."

My eyes widened. "The kitchen curtains Sharon made this spring?"

"Listen, Mel. Syl. If Mel's okay, I gotta go."

I grinned. "I'm a lot better now."

SYL INSISTED THAT HE follow me home to check the house. I didn't expect anyone to be lying in wait for me. My emotional exhaustion was doubtless the reason I didn't mind following his guidance.

Sandi and Stooper sat on the porch at the farm, and they stood as we pulled into the yard. When I called Stooper to ask him to pick up Mister Tibbs and Cat, I'd forgotten he'd have no way into the house.

Stooper got to me first and drew me into a bear hug. "Damn good thing that cat was hell bent on saving you."

Sandi nodded. "We didn't know how long you'd be, so I picked up some food for them at the dollar store. They're fine."

I nodded. "Thanks."

Cat lay stretched out on a front porch step, acting as if he owned the place. Mister Tibbs did not leave the porch. She yipped once, and I walked to her and sat on the top step to pet her.

"It'll be okay." *Not really. But you and Cat will still get fed and walked.*

I dug keys from my pocket and handed them to Sandi. "I have some beer in the fridge." I nodded at Stooper. "And some frozen lemonade you can put in a pitcher."

Stooper looked at Syl, who had leaned over to pet Cat. "She okay?"

Since I could respond myself, I said, "I'm fine. I'm not sure about Ginny Forman though."

Stooper extended a hand to pull me to my feet. "People out searching for her all over town. Hopin' she just went to visit friends or something."

The three of us, led by Mister Tibbs, walked into the house. Sandi had three beers on the counter, with the can of frozen lemonade next to them. "Why do people think she's missing or in trouble?"

I turned on the dining room light. I still had only my recliner in the living room. I really needed to buy some furniture. "Have a seat you guys."

I grabbed a beer from the counter, twisted the cap, and took a long swig. "Because Janet said some things that made it sound like Ginny was not long for this world. Or could be out of it already."

"Crud," Stooper said. "I liked her."

Sandi half-smiled. "Don't write her obit just yet. Where can we look?"

I glanced through the window at the gathering dusk. "I heard someone say they got a warrant to search Janet's home and the elevator offices. I saw a couple deputies door-knocking, when we drove through town."

Syl nodded. "And I heard Sophie on the phone, as we walked out of the sheriff's place. They're calling her folks to get a list of friends."

Sandi, Syl, and I began to seat ourselves at the table, as a scratching sound came from the front door. Cat wanted to join us.

Sandi walked to the door and let him in. "Make yourself at home." She turned to me. "What's his name, anyway?"

"He doesn't have one. I just call him Cat." Exhaustion swept over me. The adrenalin that had fueled my response to Janet Dodson had worn off.

Stooper came in from the kitchen, freshly made lemonade in hand. "Heard what he did. Needs a name."

As Syl said, "What about Rascal?" Stooper said, "I vote for Hell-Bent."

Sandi grinned. "H.B. for short."

I smiled slightly. "I'll take both under advisement."

"Whoa," Stooper said.

I shrugged. "Have to think about it."

"It's not like he'll come when you call him," Sandi said.

Stooper frowned. "So, Mel, tell us exactly what Janet Dodson believed about Ginny."

I relayed Janet's fury at an affair, as well as targeting me, thanks to Ryan, for raising questions about Tom maybe skimming money. "She said Ginny wouldn't need any more money. But you had to hear her tone, see her expression. She means to hurt her."

"No hint of a hiding place?" Stooper asked.

"Seems there would be limited places to conceal her," Syl said.

Sandi tapped a pen on her open reporter's notebook. "If she's alive. A body could be easier to conceal."

I shook my head. "I would think it would be harder for a woman Janet's size. She couldn't pick up Ginny's body."

"She could drag it," Stooper said.

Syl took a pull on his beer. "Or adopt the tried-and-true method of rolling it into a carpet."

"Not funny." I felt churlish even as I said it.

"Not saying it is. If any of you have a clue where to look, I'll drive around."

I glanced at the wall clock. "Five-thirty. It'll be close to dark in a few minutes."

Sandi pushed away from the table. "I hate to be self-serving, but I have a story to write for the paper's web page. I'll contact the sheriff and anybody else I can think of as I write. If I pick up anything, I'll call you."

I waved her away without saying anything, and Stooper stood to join her. "I know that patch of woods heading west out of town. I think I'll check out there."

"You don't live near there," Syl said.

Stooper grinned. "If I couldn't make it home from Beer Rental Heaven fast enough, I'd stop there to water the bushes."

With Stooper and Sandi gone, quiet set in. I looked at Syl. "Thanks for everything."

"I must admit, I lived in the LA area most of my life, and I never set foot in a police station. How many times have I gone to the sheriff's place with you? Or to get you?"

"A few." Why did I suddenly feel so awkward? Must be the bone-deep tiredness.

Perhaps sensing my mood, Syl asked, "You just found out your parents' deaths might not have been accidental. That's a big deal."

"It is. And I can't think of anything to do about it. Let's say Tom Dodson chased them down and ran them into the semi – even unintentionally. He might be a suspect, but he can't be punished."

"And you may never know if that's true. Maybe Janet wanted to trash talk her late, philandering husband."

I closed my eyes and rubbed a forefinger over them. "She'll protect his reputation because she has to live here. Or until she goes to jail anyway. I think what ticked her off at me was that she thought her reputation would suffer if people knew Tom hid money."

When I opened my eyes, Syl's expression surprised me. Sympathy? Did he find my thinking ludicrous, and he didn't want to say so?

He cleared his throat. "You've had a rough day. I know it's early, but you might sleep if you went to bed." He averted his gaze.

"I need to wake up. How about joining me for a walk around the barn with Mister Tibbs?"

Syl peered at her under the table, lying by my feet. "I didn't know a dog could look worried."

I stood. "From her world view, being in a truck other than mine, with Cat no less, was a major event." I slapped my thigh. "Come on girl. We'll get your leash."

Cat followed the three of us into the yard, and the crisp air made me feel more alert. Not totally, but some.

"Wouldn't Mister Tibbs walk with you even without a leash?"

"Probably, but she might not want to come in, and I don't think she knows the farm well enough to wander."

Cat dashed ahead and stopped at the corner of the barn. Since he frantically tried to get his paw under a small hole at one corner, I figured he'd gone after a mouse. Mister Tibbs strained on her leash.

Syl laughed. "You're discriminating against Mister Tibbs."

Nothing seemed funny to me at the moment, so I kept quiet.

Mister Tibbs did her business less than a foot from Cat, and it had what was undoubtedly the desired effect. Cat moved, and Mister Tibbs inspected the spot by the barn.

I sighed. "I have a feeling they're going to spend a lot of time trying to one-up each other."

We continued on our U-shaped path toward the back of the barn. I was suddenly very aware of Syl's height. And maybe his aftershave. Definitely not a farm smell.

When I stiffened, Syl said, "You okay?" He paused and faced me.

I stopped and looked up at him. "I'm okay, just…"

He bent over and kissed me lightly. No tongue, no arms wrapped around me. No fireworks, but I liked feeling the pressure of his lips on mine.

Almost in perfect sync, we faced forward, smiled, and resumed walking. My sideways glance showed Syl still smiling.

"I've been wanting to do that," he said.

"These days, I'm not sure what I want, but that was nice."

"Just nice?"

I smiled. "Somebody tried to shoot me today. Nice is good."

CHAPTER TWENTY

I CLIMBED INTO BED, alone, at seven-thirty. Syl had made us an omelet, and I hadn't felt any stress as we ate.

I'd never had a romantic partner who started out as a friend. That could make getting to know each other easier, or it could mean if the boyfriend-girlfriend thing didn't work I'd lose a friend. I pushed the thought aside as Cat leapt onto the foot of the bed.

I lifted my head a few inches. "Told you to sleep on the floor."

He stared at me as if I should know my place. Then he settled into a regal pose by my feet, a black doormat at my toes.

Mister Tibbs whimpered from the floor near my head and padded over.

"This is ridiculous." I reached down to pet her. "I'm not running a zoo, and you're too big to be up here."

After thirty seconds of head rubbing, she went back to her dog bed in the corner.

I brought to mind a spot near the river, by the town baseball diamond. I needed the gentle rush of the Des Moines River to lull me to sleep.

AT THREE-THIRTY A.M. my eyes flew open. Ginny Forman had walked into a dream. I didn't remember what I was dreaming about. Maybe nothing. Perhaps my mind simply wanted her to be found.

Since I had jerked awake, Cat moved by my feet. When he saw my open eyes, he stretched and came to my face.

"Go away," I whispered.

He sat by my cheek and rubbed it with his head. I pulled away a couple of inches. "If you hadn't saved my life, I'd smack you."

Paws on the floor announced Mister Tibbs. She gave a muted ruff.

I groaned. "I know what that means." I pushed Cat away, and he rolled on his side. He had no intention of joining Mister Tibbs and me in the pre-dawn air.

I got up and stuck my sockless feet in sneakers. "Come on. We are *not* taking a walk."

October isn't winter, but the temperature is often in the thirties at night. I grabbed a hoodie and scarf from a peg by the side door. Mister Tibbs trotted down the steps ahead of me.

Dew had moistened the grass and my sneakers squelched with each step. "We aren't walking around the barn."

Mister Tibbs picked up that this was just a potty trip and sniffed the ground around the side of the house. I considered the conversation with Janet Dodson for the umpteenth time. *No one needed to know where Ginny was, and she wouldn't need any more money.*

I hoped Sheriff Gallagher could figure out Janet's movements for much of the prior day. Had she lived on the edge of town and rarely shopped, she might not be noticed. But almost everyone knew Janet Dodson. Aside from the family business, every December she wrote a "shop locally" letter to the editor for the *South County News*. The business owners loved her.

"Come on Mister Tibbs. It's cold."

She finished doing her business and came toward me.

As I hung my hoodie back on its peg, I hoped Ginny was indoors tonight. She could die from exposure. My mind roamed the town, finally reaching the Dodson Grain Elevator complex. I pictured the silos' groupings, the older steel silos toward the back of the complex, office in front.

The office would have been easily searched. Some silos had a low-level entry door, which led to a small enclosed space in which a person could stand. An employee would use levers to operate the hydraulics to move the grain. Surely the sheriff or deputies had gotten keys and checked those spaces.

The storage space in the silos would be full this time of year. Since they were filled from the top, no way could Janet have gotten a person – dead or alive – into the grain without being seen. For miles.

Despite the Harrison Ford movie, *Witness*, people did not routinely get crushed in grain silos. But what if Janet put Ginny – or her body – in one, expecting grain to soon be poured over her? *Ugh.*

As I pushed Cat aside and climbed back into bed, I wondered if any would be empty now. Janet would certainly have any keys needed to stuff Ginny in a silo last night. But Ginny would have been missed at the library. If it had been a day she worked.

What if it had gotten too dark for the sheriff's deputies to search every part of the property? I had almost convinced myself that 'someone else' would check all the silos when Cat moved closer to my feet. They were cold from my time outside. It felt good.

What if Ginny Forman is in the cold all night?

"Nuts." I sat up and glanced at Mister Tibbs in her corner. "Want to go for a ride?"

CAT FOLLOWED US OUTSIDE. "I can't put you on a leash. You better not get lost." I wouldn't mind not having Cat. But I didn't like the idea of leaving him roaming around the grounds of the elevator in the cold as he hunted rodents.

I unlocked the pickup and helped Mister Tibbs inside, throwing the leash after her. Cat hopped in and walked across the middle console to the back seat. Mister Tibbs barked from the front passenger seat.

Usually I make her sit in back, but I wasn't about to force them to sit together. "It's your lucky day. You can ride up front."

The farm isn't too far outside of River's Edge, and I passed no other cars on the gravel roads at three thirty a.m. As we drove through town toward the elevator, on the opposite end of the town, I half expected to see sheriff deputies or others walking around. No one walked the empty streets. Maybe they had searched every outside venue late yesterday afternoon and early evening.

Cat walked into the front seat and hopped on the floor. Apparently he wanted to be near the blowing heater. "If you want it warm, you better stay in the truck when I get out."

I pulled into the grain elevator lot. After thinking for a second, I drove behind the office. No sense advertising my presence.

The glove compartment held my heavy-duty flashlight and spare batteries, though I didn't expect to need replacements. We wouldn't be here long. I fastened the leash on Mister Tibbs and got out of the truck with her. So did Cat.

The hard-packed dirt had a smattering of gravel. "Bet this is messy when it rains a lot." Even though I spoke softly, in the quiet my voice sounded like a shout.

I started toward the nearest silo, then turned toward the dumpster. Because I stopped suddenly, both animals did, too. I walked the twenty yards to it and shone my flashlight into the nearly full container.

"Whew. I don't want to go in there to look." I turned to walk toward the silos, then returned to the dumpster. The trash was all in black bags. How dirty could I get?

You're here to look for Ginny. Yes, but this will take five minutes.

I dragged Mister Tibbs back to my pickup, opened the back, and removed a long-handled rake. "We're just going to poke on the bags to see if some have a bunch of files."

Mister Tibbs led me back to the dumpster. I placed her leash on the ground and, firmly, said, "Stay."

Her eyes followed Cat, now twenty feet away.

I prodded the bags with the straight end of the rake, then used the tines to turn a couple of bags over. I didn't know the grain elevator business well enough to have expectations for the bags' contents. What I hoped to find was not just paper – I could tell there was a lot of that – but the stiffness of manila folders.

After turning over a couple of lighter-weight bags, my pole struck gold. Or at least, manila. But I couldn't move the heavy bag to me. "Crud."

The walls of the brown dumpster were less than five feet tall. But still too high for me to easily climb in. I hit on the idea of pulling out a couple lighter-weight bags to stand on, so I could scramble in. "I must be nuts."

Cat had returned to see what I was up to, and Mister Tibbs kept smelling my shoes and pawing the side of the container. She really wanted to get to the smells in there.

I took out three bags, laid them atop one another, and climbed up. When I jumped lightly into the dumpster, I sunk below the height of the bags. "Great. Squishy stuff."

I waded to the heavy bag and felt its outside. Definitely folders and paper. A lot of paper. As I hefted the bag onto the ground, Cat jumped into the dumpster.

I groaned. "Come out." I knew he wouldn't. I angled myself over the edge and back onto the ground, avoiding the bags I'd stepped on earlier. Once on firm footing, I tossed the bags back into the dumpster.

"Come on Mister Tibbs. Let's put this in the truck."

Since the bag contents were not arranged neatly, carrying it was awkward. I almost stumbled as I pushed it into the back of my truck. I shut the tailgate and wiped my hands on my jeans. "Come on, Mister Tibbs."

We had barely gone ten feet when Cat streaked by us. Mister Tibbs pulled on her leash, trying to keep up with Cat. I tugged gently. "Stay with me." She slowed, but didn't walk the ten feet back to my side.

I wasn't sure what to do except walk around every steel silo. The closest one was roughly fifty yards from the office. "I forgot how huge these suckers are." I knocked on it. Sounded full.

The door on the side was a couple of steps up, no window. I knocked on it anyway. That enclosed space was hollow, because the sound was really different than on the other part of the silo.

We checked the two silos behind the first one and I was ready to head home. "I must be nuts. It's cold out here." *And if Ginny is out here somewhere, she's really freezing.*

When I got back to the farm, I could warm up. About fifty yards separated the individual silos, with a group of three immediately next to each other. Finally, I approached the silo that sat at the greatest distance from the office. I thought it might be empty. A few spots of rust along the bottom reinforced that idea.

Suddenly, Mister Tibbs began to bark, and Cat ran toward one side of the silo.

I stooped next to Mister Tibbs and put my arm around her midriff. "Shush. It's probably a fox."

When I stood she jerked so hard the leash fell from my hand. She ran to the edge of the silo and joined Cat in smelling it.

"Quiet!"

The metallic tapping sound did not come from a fox.

LIGHTS FROM THE SHERIFF CARS and an ambulance bounced off the silver sides of the steel silos, reminding me of a light show I'd seen in college. Except those colors included more than red and blue, and loud music accompanied the lights.

Deputy Newt Harmon had used a bolt cutter to remove the lock. When he first opened the door I stood back, so had no idea what condition Ginny was in. Two EMTs had been in the silo for almost ten minutes. I couldn't hear them asking questions or getting answers. Did that mean Ginny was unconscious?

Finally, one of them called, "Ready for the gurney. Put a bigger Maglite on her."

A deputy and volunteer firefighter trundled a gurney over the uneven ground. Another deputy shone a huge flashlight into the dark silo.

When the gurney reached the small door, an EMT yelled, "We've got her on the blanket. We'll lift her out."

The woman on the blanket seemed lifeless, but then she moved her head slightly. At my side, Mister Tibbs barked, and she twisted her head enough to see me.

I gave her a thumbs up gesture and thought I saw a faint smile before she closed her eyes. As the gurney passed near me, an EMT said, "Sorry about the bumpy ride, Ginny."

I realized he was John, Ambrose's good friend who had transported me one time. His eyes met mine, and he shook his head. But he smiled, so I figured Ginny's condition wasn't grave.

Cold permeated me, starting with my feet. I turned, hoping to be allowed to drive home, but knowing that would be wishful thinking.

Sheriff Gallagher's voice came from behind me. "Melanie." He wore blue jeans and a stocking cap. His parka made me jealous.

"Happy to talk to you, but I'm really cold."

He nodded. "Come on down to the office. I'll make you coffee and even let you bring in your dog."

I glanced around. "I also have a black cat. Somewhere."

"Jeez. Patel got you to take it?"

"How come everyone in town but me knew he was trying to find him a home?"

"You're a sucker. Walk around for a minute. I bet he comes up to you." He turned toward his car. "Leave your cat in your truck."

My cat.

UNLIKE ITS USUAL SPARTAN condition, Gallagher's office had empty coffee cups, a box of donuts, and a bag of potato chips. A county map covered much of the table, and a bunch of spots were circled. They must have been working through the night.

I accepted tea from a distracted-looking Newt. Coffee would have given me jitters on an empty stomach.

Mister Tibbs now lay at my feet. For the first few minutes, I'd let her sniff around the office, then I'd insisted she sit. She stood on her back legs and put a paw on my thigh.

"You're fine. Be glad you're in here and not with Cat in the truck."

Gallagher walked in. "Found him, huh?"

"Mister Tibbs did. Will Ginny be okay?"

"Mild hypothermia and a big knot on her head, back of her skull. Probably get her airlifted to Iowa City, to be safe."

"How did Janet get her in there?"

Gallagher shook his head. "Not totally sure. Ginny said something about Janet visiting her at home and something in her tea. Ginny's tea. She remembers Janet helping her with her coat and then walking out with her. Then nothing."

"So...Thursday evening?"

"Seems likely, Melanie. Ginny isn't one-hundred percent lucid."

"I feel so bad for her." Part of me didn't. Have an affair with a married man, and you open yourself up to all kinds of bad karma. Shouldn't get you killed, though.

"You're the reason she's alive." He sat behind his desk and studied me. "What in blazes made you go out there? We'd searched the office and grounds just before dark. Including walking around that empty silo. Workers said it hadn't been opened in years. They didn't even have a key to the lock hanging on it."

I wondered if it was the silo that had been empty when my dad was studying costs at the elevator. "Couldn't sleep, couldn't stop thinking about Ginny." I scratched Mister Tibbs' head. "If she hadn't needed a whiz, I might not have awakened enough to care to head out."

Gallagher's phone rang, and he picked it up. "Yeah." After listening for a moment, he had a thin smile, then hung up.

I stared at him.

Gallagher smiled grimly. "Janet Dodson seems not to remember that Ginny Forman ever worked for the grain elevator."

I snorted. "I seem to recall she yelled that Ginny was a bitch when she heard me say the name."

Gallagher rubbed his hands over his eyes and glanced at me. "I remember that, too."

"I assume she's your only suspect for how Ginny got in that silo?"

Gallagher shrugged. "Far as I'm concerned, but she and her lawyer may have other theories."

"Didn't Ginny tap when you guys searched there earlier?" I asked.

He shook his head. "About the only things she said besides thanks and a mumble about tea was that she just woke up. Lucky she had on a winter coat."

I had given him a brief statement and didn't see what else to add. "Can I go home now?"

"Lemme see if I can read my notes." He read silently for perhaps thirty seconds, then looked up. "Sure. If you're lucky your reporter friends will let you sleep."

CHAPTER TWENTY-ONE

I DIDN'T WAKE UP SATURDAY until eight-thirty. I wouldn't have awakened then except the house phone in the kitchen rang. I stumbled into the kitchen brightness and answered.

"Melanie? It's Sandi. You didn't answer your cell."

"I turned it off so I could sleep."

"So you were at the elevator when they found Ginny?"

"Actually, Cat and Mister Tibbs found her."

"What?!"

I gave her the thirty-second version. "I need to make coffee and walk Mister Tibbs."

"I'm coming out there. You want me to pick up egg sandwiches at the diner?"

I yawned. "Good idea."

Mister Tibbs had not had her usual amount of beauty sleep, so she was content to water the grass near the house. Cat watched from his window.

By the time Sandi arrived, I had showered and dried my hair. It was the first time I'd felt truly warm since before I left for the grain elevator earlier that morning.

I put the tea kettle on the burner as Sandi walked in. "That bag of food smells great. Thanks a lot."

She put the sandwiches on the counter and opened my fridge. "You need to buy some juice."

"Thanks, Mom."

She grinned. "Everyone in the diner was talking about it. They say Ginny wouldn't have lasted much longer if you hadn't found her."

"I'm really glad I did. We did." I picked up my sandwich, some napkins, and my coffee and headed for the dining room table. "Fix your tea and come in here."

She joined me as I finished half of the sandwich. "Is your cell phone still off?"

"Oh, right. Did you try to call again while you were driving out here?"

She nodded her head toward a window. "No, but Syl must have tried. His truck is pulling into your yard."

I took my phone out of my purse and walked toward the front door as I turned on the ringer. "Save me telling about it twice."

Syl kissed me on the cheek as he walked in. Sandi dropped part of her sandwich on the floor. Mister Tibbs grabbed it and ran to the kitchen.

I grinned and turned to Syl. "Coffee in the kitchen."

He looked at Sandi. "Were you with her last night?"

She shook her head. "Just the two ornery animals."

As Syl poured his coffee in the kitchen, Sandi mouthed, "What is that about?"

I ignored her and sat down as Syl came in and joined us. "Why didn't you call me?"

I shrugged. "I only went out there because I couldn't sleep."

"That's what you get for going to bed so early," he said.

Sandi's eyes widened. "Give us the whole scoop, Mel."

I did, without mentioning the bag of trash. I'd only just remembered it.

Neither of them said anything for several seconds.

Finally, Sandi asked, "So, we can be certain Janet put her in the silo, maybe after drugging her? But we don't know when."

"Or why no one saw her," Syl said.

I nodded. "That is odd. But the crops are harvested, so I don't think the elevator offices open until nine. And it's on the edge of town. She could have put her there late Thursday or real early Friday."

Sandi drained her tea. "Ground's pretty hard. She could have driven Ginny right up to the door of that empty silo."

I shrugged. "And rolled her out of the car, or maybe told her to walk in there if she didn't want to get shot or something."

"Doesn't make sense," Syl said. "She could have screamed all day."

"It's at the back of the property." I thought for a moment. "I wonder if she was gagged? When I got there, she tapped, not yelled. Oh, and she said something to the sheriff about just waking up."

"Still doesn't tell us who killed Tom," Sandi said. "Janet was in the Farm Bureau dinner the entire time he was out of the room."

I nodded, slowly. "Janet said Tom came back to her. And that he had given money to Ginny. Maybe she was mad he stopped. In fact, Janet pretty much said she thinks Ginny killed Tom."

Sandi gave me a withering look. "Important detail, Mel."

I grinned. "The skills I forget."

"This Ginny wasn't at the dinner, was she?" Syl asked.

"She wasn't," Sandi said. "But no one else was in that hallway to see her, or anyone else who killed Dodson."

I balled up my sandwich wrapping. "But what are the odds that Tom happened to walk out there, and she happened to be there?"

"Maybe they planned to meet," Sandi said.

"And she brought a circular weapon to off him?" I asked.

Syl frowned. "What circular weapon?"

Sandi repeated what the autopsy report had said about a semi-circle indentation in Tom's head.

"I'm going to ask Mrs. Reilly if there had been a box of canned goods down there. Maybe even in the closet."

Sandi studied me. "I don't recall seeing a box."

I thought for a moment. "It's all kind of a blur. But if a box didn't have a lot in it, a killer could have taken it when she, or he, ran out."

"So," Syl said, "she didn't plan to kill him, but maybe just grabbed what was close? Aren't there any cameras down there?"

"The only camera on church property faces the parking lot, near the main doors. Even if Ginny took the box, it still doesn't explain how they ran into each other." I paused. "Sheriff said they might transfer her to Iowa City. I wonder if they did that?"

Sandi stood. "I should be able to find out."

Syl grinned at me. "Keeps you from getting on Gallagher's bad side. Again."

"Or Ambrose's...damn. I better call him."

Sandi stood. "I'll talk to you later, Mel." She almost scampered out the front door.

I was beginning to feel like a little kid who had to report her whereabouts to parents, so they knew where to find her after school.

When I finished dialing, I glanced at Syl.

He smiled. "I can guess what you were thinking. He does own half the farm, right?"

I recognized my tone as grudging. "He does."

"Of course, if you'd stay out of trouble...," he began.

Ambrose's tone belied humor, and he didn't bother to say hello. "So, Mel, I suppose I could say only call when you're in trouble, but I'd be on the phone a lot."

Syl heard Ambrose's words and laughed. Maybe I could turn the volume down on the cell phone receiver.

"Morning, Syl," Ambrose said.

"Ditto," Syl said.

I knew how to one-up Ambrose. "You never said how much trouble you got into because the goat ate Sharon's curtain."

"Sheesh. A lot. She blames me, because I'm the one who left the window open."

I grinned. "Good for her. Anyway, I'm okay, and I think we got to Ginny in time. Who told you?"

Syl leaned down to pet Mister Tibbs, and Ambrose said, "I have my sources."

I thought I knew at least one of them. "Anyway, Sandi's writing a story for the paper's web page. I bet it'll have more than I know."

Ambrose chuckled. "If you're trying to get me off the phone, that's fine. When Sharon gets back from the grocery store, she may want to know more. You are okay, right?"

"It turned out well so, yes, thanks."

"Then I gotta run. I have to milk the goats and take the stuff to that parenting place."

I hung up and answered the question in Syl's eyes by explaining that the milk was for babies who couldn't drink cows' milk.

"Ah." Syl grinned. "That explains why he's still allowed to keep them." He glanced at his watch. "I'm finishing a summary report for a client." His face reddened slightly. "Where does one go to a movie around here?"

I grinned. "One goes to Fairfield, but Ottumwa has more choices."

He stood and pointed a finger at me. "Smarty. Call you about dinner time?"

"Sure." I walked him to the door, but neither of us leaned in for a kiss. *We have to figure out the logistics of this.* As Syl left, I moved farther into the house, but watched his truck leave the yard.

A week ago, just one week, we'd gone to the Farm Bureau dinner together. Tonight we seemed to have an actual date.

And I still didn't know for sure who killed Tom Dodson.

I APPLIED MAKEUP, telling myself I wanted to perk up after a night with little sleep. The clock showed only nine-thirty. Sandi hadn't called, but maybe I could find out which hospital had Ginny and visit. I thought it unlikely she had been arrested based on Janet's ramblings. Having an affair wasn't a crime.

After walking Mister Tibbs and being ignored by Cat, I took the black garbage sack out of my truck and carried it to the spare bedroom at the back of the first floor. Sitting on the hardwood floor in the empty room, the contents became a beacon for curious eyes.

With my animals watching, I opened the bag and began removing file folders, some of which contained bank statements, loose paperwork, and a few empty coffee cups.

I studied the labels on the folders. They seemed to deal more with the Dodsons' personal finances than the business.

I didn't really care about the family's household budget. Plus, the bank statements listed the check numbers and amounts, not what they were for.

As I reached to the bottom of the bag, Cat leapt from his spot several feet away and landed in the sack. "Hey! This isn't a game."

To him, it was. I tried to lift Cat out, but he burrowed further. Mister Tibbs stuck his head around my elbow to look in.

"This is ridiculous." I pushed Mister Tibbs back and reached to the bottom of the bag. My fingers closed around what could only be a pill bottle. I shook it as I removed it, but it was empty. The label remained. Gabapentin!

I reached over to hug Mister Tibbs, and yelled, "She did it. She definitely started that fire!"

Mister Tibbs shook her head and backed away a couple of feet.

"Okay, sorry I yelled, girl." I sat the pill bottle on the floor next to me, and Mister Tibbs came close to smell it.

Next, I removed a brown, accordion-style envelope folder. In magic marker, the front flap said **Corn Yields**. A rubber band broke with a snap as I took it off. The noise made Mister Tibbs back away a couple of feet, but Cat's movements returned her attention to the bag.

The files in the accordion envelope had nothing to do with corn yields. They appeared to be a separate bank account, in Tom's name only, and the bank was in Keosauqua, not River's Edge. This account had torn cancelled checks. The checks struck me as odd. I wasn't sure my bank even offered to send them anymore.

The account had been used relatively little compared to the joint account. Statements showed that two or three times per month, someone deposited two to five thousand dollars.

The cancelled checks for the Keosauqua account had been torn into tiny strips and placed in the box with unused checks. Though I could see the dollar amount for checks in the statements, if I wanted to know to whom checks were written, I'd need concentrated time to go through the pieces. Not now.

My sense was that this second account showed how Tom Dodson spent some of the money he skimmed. Perhaps, by labeling it **Corn Yields**, he figured Janet would never look at it.

If she had found it and then wanted to discard it, the company dumpster seemed as good a resting place as any. But my bet was she never opened the material.

I decided to keep only the accordion envelope. I shoved the bank items and pill bottle into it and stuffed it at the back of a shelf in my bedroom closet. But what to do with the other contents of the sack?

I giggled. Not my burn barrel. I had the same problem Janet had with files that belonged to my father. If these were found in my possession, how would I explain them?

"Nuts." I took Cat out of the bag. He offered no protest, and walked away with his tail in the air, Mister Tibbs following.

I put the material about the Dodsons' household finances back in the bag, carried it to the basement, and stuck it in a dark corner behind some old plywood. I went upstairs, put dry food in the animals' bowls, and climbed in my truck to drive to the hospital.

River's Edge is lucky to have the twenty-five-bed health center. It has some kind of funding arrangement for rural hospitals that enables it to stay solvent. A town that loses its hospital gets a lot smaller pretty fast.

Usually I went in a side door, but today I walked to the front desk to ask about Ginny. I fully expected to be told she was not a patient, but it turned out she had not been transferred to a bigger facility.

The elderly volunteer at the front desk consulted a note taped to her phone. "I need to call the floor to see if you can go up. I told a couple other people she didn't want visitors, but the nurse said she might later."

"Sure, tell them it's Melanie."

The expression of the volunteer, whose name was Garnet, indicated she thought I was full of myself, so I added, "I'm the one who saved her last night." An exaggeration, but the woman's expression and posture indicated she was now on my side.

I moved away so the volunteer would think I couldn't hear her press my case.

She cupped her hand around the mouthpiece and lowered her voice. After being on hold for almost a minute, she listened some more and smiled. "Thanks. I'll send her up."

Big smile to me. "They asked her if you could come up. She hasn't wanted other visitors. Anyway, she said yes. Room 314."

Big smile back to her. "Thank you, Garnet."

The elevator came at once, and I pondered what to say as I rode to the third floor, the only one with patient rooms. I had no intention of asking Ginny if she killed Dodson. I simply wanted to explore whether Janet was correct in accusing the former accountant of having an affair with Tom. Once I knew that, I'd decide if I needed to learn more myself or leave it to Gallagher and crew.

Why did I care?

Because maybe Dodson was responsible for my parents' deaths. Would he have talked to Ginny about that the way he seemed to have talked to Janet?

Ginny's room was at the far end of the hallway to the right of the elevator. I passed a small sitting room for family members, nodded at the lone nurse in the nurses' station, and admired the clean tile floor.

A night's sleep, food, and fluids can do wonders for a person. Ginny lay in a bed with its head raised. An IV still flowed, but without it I might have thought she had slept in her own bed last night rather than on a silo floor.

She smiled and pointed to a chair next to the bed. "My hero."

I sat and shook my head slightly. "The cat and dog heard your taps before I did."

Her eyes widened. "I didn't know that. I don't remember a whole lot before I got here."

"Bad time for you. I half-expected that you had been transferred to Iowa City or someplace."

"I didn't want to go." She frowned and pointed an index finger at herself. "That woman is not running me out of town."

I grinned. "Or me either. Did you hear she came after me with a rifle yesterday?"

Ginny stared at me for several seconds. "No one told me that."

"Actually, we both owe my pets a lot." I relayed a condensed version of Janet's visit to Syl's place.

Ginny shook her head slightly and winced. "They say if I have a concussion, it's just a mild one. I hope they let me go today." She studied me. "That woman really is insane."

"Don't rush it. I hear the food's improved a lot through the years."

She smiled. "Supposedly I get a regular lunch today."

I decided to appear confused. "I understand why she'd be irritated that my dad thought Tom was skimming money, but it's not like I was on that dumb advisory committee."

Ginny glanced out the window and back to me. "And it's not like your father could make that point now. I mean, oh, goodness. That was tactless."

"Not a problem. Plus, it's a valid point."

From the hallway came Gallagher's voice. "She in the same room?"

Ginny whispered. "I don't think I'm supposed to talk to a lot of people."

I grinned and whispered, "I have an idea." I raised my voice to a normal tone and picked up a pen and napkin from her tray table. "Okay, so you'd like a nightgown and undies."

She caught on immediately. "And I don't need all my makeup, but if you could get the blush-on in the bathroom…Oh, hi, sheriff."

I turned and gave Gallagher a brilliant smile. "She looks good, doesn't she?"

He took in both of us and nodded. "Came to see for yourself?"

"I figured she might be here for a while, so I could bring her some of her things…"

He interrupted me, but looked at Ginny. "For another day or so your house is a crime scene, so maybe Mel can pick up a couple things at the store for you."

Ginny looked as if she might cry, but something told me it was an act.

"I can get a couple things in town, but I'm happy to drive over to Keosauqua. Or Fairfield. They have that Walmart."

Still with a bit of a trembling lip, she said, "I wanted to go home."

Gallagher smiled and pulled up the room's second chair. "You didn't see how you looked last night, Ginny. Another day of rest and doctoring will do you good." He turned to me. "Why don't you take that drive, Melanie?"

He didn't say "get the hell out," but it was implied.

CHAPTER TWENTY-TWO

BEFORE I DROVE TO FAIRFIELD, I picked up Mister Tibbs and Cat. They had earned the right to spend the day riding with me. I even let Mister Tibbs hang her head out the window when we drove from the farm to town. Once we were on Highway 1, I pulled her and her wagging tongue into the truck.

I rarely venture beyond nearby towns, and today I would go to Fairfield once and either there or Ottumwa this evening for a movie. I supposed I could have gotten clothes for Ginny at the Dollar General in Keosauqua, but though I'd bought some essentials there for myself, she didn't seem like the Dollar General type.

As I drove north, I thought about why the sheriff's deputies would need to be in Ginny's house today. I got that they might be looking for Janet's fingerprints or something, but what else?

Maybe Janet told Gallagher that Ginny had been the recipient of not only Tom Dodson's affections but some of the company's money.

I thought Gallagher owed me a conversation about what he would do with Janet Dodson. He would almost certainly disagree.

Halfway to Fairfield I slowed for what locals would still call a town and anyone driving through would resent as a silly place to drop speed from fifty-five to thirty-five. As younger residents left rural towns, once-thriving hardware stores, diners, and eventually churches evaporated. The only reminders of formerly vibrant small towns were a blinking traffic light, ten or so houses, and maybe a working soda machine at the sole remaining business in town – usually a car repair shop.

Unlike a couple of shrinking towns south of it, Fairfield thrived. While I was in Walmart, I bought a bunch of bags of topsoil, much cheaper than at the River's Edge hardware store, and some flea medicine, litter, and food for Cat.

I didn't put a lot of thought into what to get for Ginny. Two simple nightgowns, a three-pack of cotton underwear, and some blush-on.

If she was a murderer, she'd get her clothes provided at the state prison in Fort Madison, or wherever. In the meantime, I had the excuse of the nightgowns to get me back into her room in the late afternoon. Unless Sheriff Gallagher left specific orders that I not be allowed to see her.

Back in my truck, Mister Tibbs and Cat were glad to see me. Mister Tibbs, anyway. Cat made a show of ignoring me by remaining curled in the back seat. He opened one eye and quickly closed it when I grinned at him. "See, you do care."

Sandi called as I neared River's Edge. I put her on speaker. "Yes, Madam Reporter."

"Hey. You saw Ginny. What did you find out?"

"You have good spies. Not much. Gallagher stopped by not long after I got there."

"Rats. I tried sneaking up to her room, but the door's shut and a nurse shooed me away."

I sped up to pass an aged Chrysler LeBaron sedan going thirty miles per hour. "I have an excuse to go back. Gallagher told her she couldn't get into her house today, and I told her I'd pick up some nightgowns and undies for her."

"See, you do know something!"

"He told her the house was still a crime scene. I don't know what they expect to find."

"Huh. Maybe I'll wander over there."

"You should find somebody in the sheriff's office to date."

"Funny. You haven't mentioned why Syl kissed you when he came to your house this morning."

Thankfully, Sandi couldn't see me blush. "Not a big deal."

"And?"

"No 'and,' Sandi. He's been really good to me. In fact, he made me an omelet before he left last night."

"And did you eat it before or after?"

"Stop already. It's not like that."

"I'll stop, for now. You want to go to supper this evening?"

"I, uh, think I might be going to a movie with Syl."

She laughed. "I won't stop. Call me if you find out more from Ginny."

TWENTY MINUTES LATER, I pulled into the hospital parking lot. Parts were shaded, so I left Mister Tibbs and Cat in the truck with the windows cracked two inches. I was more concerned they would be cold than hot in the forty-eight degree temperature, but reminded myself they had fur coats.

No one sat in the small hospital lobby. Late afternoon on a Saturday didn't even merit a welcome volunteer. A sign on the reception desk said, "Dial zero for assistance."

When I exited the elevator on the third floor, Ryan nodded from his spot leaning against the wall opposite the elevator.

I stopped rather than have him follow me. "If you're looking for me, you've got a lot of nerve."

He shrugged. "Janet Dodson's the one who drew conclusions about what you know."

"You're the one who put possibly unrelated facts together. Go talk to Janet." I walked past him.

"Come on, Mel. You've talked to Ginny. How did Janet get her into that silo?"

"Leave me alone, Ryan."

He didn't follow.

As I neared the door to Ginny's room, I slowed my pace and took a couple of deeper breaths. If I walked in there looking out of sorts, she might talk less.

A woman called to me from the nurse's station. "Ms. Perkins. The sheriff said five minutes."

I took in her chin-length blonde hair and navy-blue scrubs as I stopped and held up the Walmart bag. "Won't take that long to give her these. How's she doing?"

"I can't discuss her condition, but I'd say she feels a lot better than when she arrived here." She smiled, which made her look younger than the forty years I'd pegged her for. "She's lucky you found her."

I returned the smile. "My cat and dog did."

"Handy pets."

I nodded and walked to Ginny's door and knocked lightly. I opened it an inch and identified myself.

"Come on in, Melanie."

I shut the door behind me and was surprised to see her wipe tears from her cheeks. "You okay, Ginny?"

She straightened the blanket on her bed. "I'm fine. I just want to go home. I don't understand why my house is still a crime scene."

I sat in the chair next to her bed. "Not that it's my business, but if Janet took you from there, they might need to look for fingerprints and stuff."

She lowered her voice. "But they got a warrant! That means they can look anywhere."

It sure does. "I bet it's common practice. Try not to worry about it." I held up the bag. "I went high-fashion for you."

She blew her nose. "Perfect for here." She took it and peered in. "What do I owe you?"

"Wasn't even twenty-five dollars. You can buy me breakfast at the diner one day. Or not."

She pulled out the nightgowns. "Thanks. I love yellow." She sighed. "Janet stopped by Thursday night and said she came to bury the hatchet."

It seemed Ginny assumed I knew she and Tom had been lovers.

Ginny shook her head. "I was so naïve. In so many ways. I actually thought." She began to tear up. "That he loved me."

I tried to sound sympathetic. "He was probably fond of you. They have a daughter. Maybe family ties kind of pulled him back." *Or better judgment.*

She had taken out the pack of undies and kind of threw them halfway down the bed. "I think Janet figured out something was up."

It seemed odd that she would talk to me so much. She must have girlfriends. Or maybe not in town. She didn't grow up in River's Edge. On the other hand, I had pretty much saved her life.

"It may sound harsh, but he must have been into something that led someone to want to kill him. You may have been lucky not to have hung around with him after a certain point."

Ginny glanced out the window and back to me. "You could be right."

A knock and whoosh announced the nurse, who had given me the five-minute limit. "Ms. Perkins, we don't want to wear out Ms. Forman."

I stood and smiled down at Ginny. "You have guardian angels while you're in here."

Ginny gestured to the nightgowns. "Thanks so much."

I edged toward the door, which the nurse held open. "If you need anything else, you can call me."

Ginny frowned. "I don't think I have your number."

I'd left my purse in the car, so I took the black marker from a cup next to the white board on the wall at the foot of the bed, and wrote my cell number in small print. "Bet this nice nurse will give you a piece of paper to write that on."

Ms. Blue Scrubs smiled. "Sure thing. Then I'll erase your number."

Ginny waved with little enthusiasm, and I walked out with the nurse. When we were a couple doors down from Ginny's room, I said, "She looks a bit better, but kind of down. Does she have family or someone to visit?"

She nodded. "Her parents were here a couple of hours ago."

Something in the nurse's tone told me Ginny's mother and father weren't too happy about what their daughter had gotten herself into. I wondered if they would verify that Ginny had visited them the weekend Tom was murdered.

AFTER WE DISCUSSED MOVIE options, Syl stopped by at five-thirty. I told him I had a fun place for us to eat before we left town.

Juanita Sparks' barbeque place is popular. By six o'clock, all of the ten tables, with their red-and-white checkered tablecloths, are full.

For some reason, most people call her Momma Sparks. She's originally from Eastern Europe. Her English is good, but I think her unnatural sentence structure and occasional malapropisms are for effect.

Only three of the ten tables were occupied, and I guided Syl and me to one by a window. "The food is really good." As we sat, I added, "You'll want to tuck a napkin under your chin. It's moist."

Juanita walked up as I finished talking, and studied Syl. "I don't know you."

He nodded to her. "My first time. Melanie tells me you have some of the best food in town."

"I have the best." She turned to me. "You want usual pork sandwich with coleslaw?"

"Yes, but how about a menu for my friend Syl Seaton?"

"I get." She ambled the thirty feet to a table by the entry door and came back with one, which she plopped in front of Syl. "All good, but barbeque the best."

He picked up the menu. "How did you decide to specialize in barbeque?"

Mama Sparks shrugged. "You put anything in. No one know what."

I didn't grin until Mama Sparks had almost reached the kitchen. Syl didn't. "How often do you get sick from eating here?"

"Never. I do stick to her standard pork barbeque."

Syl had been studying the menu, but closed it. "Guess I'll go with that, too."

WE WERE HALFWAY TO Fairfield when the stomach cramps hit.

When I decided I couldn't wait for the movie theater, I said, "I could use a rest stop at that gas station on the left."

Syl put on his turn signal. "Good idea."

We said nothing as we walked, quickly, to our respective bathrooms. I hunted for Pepto Bismol, when I returned to the convenience store area.

Syl already stood in the same aisle. He lifted his eyebrows as he grabbed a bottle. "First time for everything."

I reached for it. "Should be my treat."

He held onto it and shook his head. "No Michelin star for Mama Sparks."

"Sorry. You still okay for the movie?"

"Should know by the time we pull into Fairfield." He grinned. "And we'll know each other a lot better."

We swigged pink liquid from different sides of the bottle, and I did feel much better before we reached the town. "If you want to drive around for a minute, I'll show you some of the hot spots."

We drove through the town square, its gazebo festooned in fall colors, and I pointed out several businesses, then the local newspaper office, which is in a brick building off the square.

By the time we had passed the third Indian restaurant and second Chinese place, Syl said, "And why did we eat with your buddy Mama Sparks?"

I shrugged. "Local color."

He grunted. "I haven't been up here. Why is it so, I don't know, cosmopolitan?"

"It's the headquarters for the TM Movement. Transcendental Meditation. People moved here from all over, starting in maybe the late '70s or '80s."

"Seems like the place to be on a Saturday night. Unlike the Farm Bureau, probably no murders."

I pointed to a parking spot on the side street we'd just turned onto. "It's only two blocks to the theater from here. Good night for a walk."

Because the temperature had dropped to the low forties, we strode at a brisk pace. "You come up here a lot?" Syl asked.

"Not too often. If I want a night on the town, I'm more likely to drive farther, to Iowa City, and meet some of my college friends."

I glanced sideways at Syl's profile. Without using the word, last week he had essentially said he was bored in River's Edge. Fairfield was only a twenty-five-mile drive. Maybe he'd decide to hang out here. "There's a good bookstore with a coffee shop. We can come up some other time."

When we reached the theater, I started to pull out my wallet. Syl shook his head. "Dinner was fine to split, but the movie was my idea."

THE DRIVE BACK TO RIVER'S EDGE dragged on. We had exhausted our discussion of the Tom Hanks movie, and Syl wasn't used to the road and its lack of street lights. Not that he said that. I ascribed his fluctuating speed to the various curves.

We pulled into the yard in front of the farmhouse at ten-thirty. Likely early by west coast date standards. I turned to Syl. "I don't have anything as fancy as a nightcap, but would you like some tea or a beer?"

He put his truck in park and nodded toward the house. "Look at your front window."

Cat and Mister Tibbs sat side by side on his chair, clearly expecting us to come in.

"I'm sure my welcoming committee would let you in."

He grinned. "One step at a time."

We leaned toward each other and kissed. More than a quick goodnight, but not yet a promise of things to come. If I even wanted that.

We pulled apart, and I smiled. "I haven't done this in a while either."

"And I don't want to blow it," Syl said.

Agreed.

CHAPTER TWENTY-THREE

I GO TO OUR METHODIST Church less than half the time. This crisp, sunny Sunday I wanted to look for the box that usually held cans for the town food pantry.

I entered by the side door and moved down the steps to the basement. Laughter and the raised voice of a teacher came from one of the Sunday School classrooms. The only two words I could discern were "sit quietly."

No box for canned goods in the hallway at the foot of the stairs. I turned right toward the community room and almost ran into a large cardboard box on which were pasted pictures of canned goods, bread, ice cream and more. A note penned on the front in magic marker said, "Let's replenish the food pantry box."

A woman's voice behind me said, "Melanie? You looking for something?" I turned. Mrs. Reilly stood just outside her office, hands holding copies of the church's weekly bulletin.

"I was going to head down to the community room to take another look for my sweater, but I suppose someone would have turned it in."

Her look told me she doubted my explanation. I walked toward her. "Can I help you carry something upstairs?"

I fell into step beside her as she shook her head. "Do you like our new box for the food pantry?"

"More decorative than the old one. Who got creative?"

"The older Sunday School class. The old box disappeared."

Bingo. "I hope whoever took it really needed the food."

She shrugged as we mounted the steps at the far end of the hallways. "Could have been taken by the sheriff when they were investigating. I meant to ask."

I didn't mention that Sandi and I thought it was gone before the sheriff and crew got there.

Mrs. Reilly and I reached the top, and I opened the door so she could enter the sanctuary ahead of me. "I usually sit toward the back."

She smiled. "Always room at the front, but it's harder to duck out."

I BARELY LISTENED TO the service. I considered not staying, since I had learned what I wanted. I decided since I'd walked in the side door it would be rude to simply walk out the back.

When it came time for the minister to ask if anyone needed 'special prayers,' Eliza Wright stood. "We've had a lot of sadness in town lately, starting with Tom Dodson's murder and, it seems, Janet Dodson's attacks on perhaps two other residents."

The room buzzed for a few seconds. The paper wouldn't be out until Monday, and not everyone read its web page or would have picked up the story on the Quincy TV station. If they even covered Janet's transgressions.

Eliza continued. "I hope Janet's actions came out of grief, but no matter what, I ask that we pray for her, Miss Ginny Forman, and our own Melanie Perkins."

Someone patted my shoulder, and I half-turned to see Ambrose's friend John and his wife Polly. I nodded. I didn't think Eliza knew I was in the building, and I now had no intention of staying until the service ended.

As we rose for the final hymn, I moved by two people to get to the side aisle. John gave me the peace sign, and Polly patted his arm, not too gently.

Outside, I took a couple deep breaths of fall air and started for the parking lot. I made it out of the lot as the doors opened and attendees began spilling out. I had intended to go home, but instead turned toward the hospital.

I could tell Ginny I wanted to know if she needed anything and mention I'd been to church. Throw in a reference to the cute food donation box the kids had just made. See if she blanched at the mention of a box that held cans-cum-weapons.

THE HOSPITAL BOASTED MORE visitors than yesterday, or perhaps it was simply because I had arrived earlier. When I got off the elevator on Ginny's floor, food smells wafted toward me. The tall metal cart that brought meals sat in the middle of the hallway.

As I drew closer to Ginny's room, its door opened and a frowning couple in their mid-fifties or so exited, shutting the door behind them. Assuming they were her parents, Ginny got her high cheekbones from her mother and her coloring from her father.

"Ridiculous that she won't move back," the man said.

The woman nodded at me and said, "Good afternoon."

I said the same, and the man bobbed his head, too. Apparently the woman's greeting had been in part to encourage her husband not to discuss family matters so publicly.

Rather than let them see me enter Ginny's room, I stopped at the nurses' station and pretended to search for something in my purse. The elevator dinged, and I glanced down the hall in time to see the door close on Ginny's still frowning visitors.

A nurse in her early fifties looked up from what she had been writing. "Need something?"

"No. I thought I brought a card for Ginny, but I guess I didn't."

"Your timing is good. She's going home in less than an hour."

"Great news. I'll see if she needs a ride."

I walked the short distance to Ginny's room and knocked. No response, so I said, "It's Melanie."

In a voice that belied either a cold or crying spell, she said, "Come on in." She blew her nose as I walked in.

I decided not to comment on the tears. "Heard you're going home today. Do you need a ride?"

She shook her head. "Sheriff Gallagher said one of the deputies would take me. They want me to look over the house to be sure nothing's missing."

I sat in the chair next to her bed. "Do they think someone broke in?"

Ginny got out of bed and walked to the built-in closet on the side of the room. "I don't think so, but they said Janet could have been in there. She had my keys after…you know."

"If the sheriff looked around, I hope it's not messy."

She shrugged as she pulled out a pair of grey slacks, which had a plastic bag over them. "I don't even care. I just want to be in my own place." As she removed the plastic, a price tag came into view.

These clothes appeared nicer than what they sell at Walmart. "A nice gift."

She rolled her eyes at me and pulled out a dark burgundy knit top, similarly ensconced in plastic. "My parents. Conservative outfit. Like my mother's."

"Beats what you wore in here."

She stared at me for a second and laughed. "I guess it's all perspective."

I had to agree with that. *At least she has parents.*

If I couldn't take her home, this might be my only chance to talk to her for a couple of days. "So, I go to the Methodist Church…"

Ginny winced.

"… and Eliza Wright stood up to ask people to pray for you and me. You might get some calls when you get home."

She paused as she picked up a comb from the bedside table. "Just what I need."

"I'm not anxious to talk to a lot of people either. It gave the congregation something positive to do. Hard to think of a murder at our church. The culprit even stole our food pantry donation box."

Ginny dropped her comb, but picked it up and concentrated on fixing her hair. "That's terrible."

"Listen, I hate to ask, but you worked in accounting at the elevator. Before someone, probably Janet, burned my dad's old files, I read them. Looked as if he thought someone might be fudging utility costs at Dodson Elevator. Do you know anything about that?"

She bit onto the tiny piece of plastic that attached the price tag to her slacks and yanked its end, so the tag came off. Without looking at me, she asked, "Does that matter now?"

"I suppose not. Janet kind of implied Tom was angry with my father and may have even run him off the road the night my folks died." When Ginny sank onto a chair near the closet, I added, "He might not have meant to."

"I don't know anything about any of that." She stood and, still wearing one of the nightgowns I bought her, pulled up the slacks.

"Nothing to be done now, anyway." I wasn't going to get anything out of her and sensed she might be upset enough to ask me to leave. I went to neutral territory. "I hope the library has good sick leave."

She removed the burgundy top from its hanger and took off the hospital gown. She wore no bra, so I averted my eyes while she drew the pullover over her head.

"The library director called. She said to take as much time as I needed." Her thin smile showed no humor. "She didn't mention whether they would pay me."

A sharp rap on the door preceded a man's voice. "Miss Forman?"

In a low voice she said, "Good timing." Louder, she added, "Come on in."

Aaron Granger entered, his eyes traveling from Ginny to me. "Good morning, ladies." As Ginny folded her gown, he pretty much gave me the stink eye.

I smiled. "I came by to see if Ginny needed a ride home."

Unsmiling, he said, "I'm her taxi today."

I stood and directed my words to Ginny. "I think you have my cell number. If you need food or something, feel free to call."

Ginny's smile appeared genuine. "Thanks for picking up the nightgowns yesterday."

"You bet." I nodded at Granger and walked out.

I RETURNED TO THE FARM and walked Mister Tibbs around the barn. When we got to the foot of the front steps, she balked at coming up.

"Hmm. I think Cat's pretty savvy. If he'll come outside, you can stay here with him." She thumped her tail and cocked her head.

I dropped her leash and walked up the steps. A thump told me Cat had jumped to the floor from his chair, and when I opened the door he darted out. I followed him down the steps and stooped to remove Mister Tibbs' leash. "Stay in the front yard only."

Mister Tibbs turned to run toward the barn. Cat tried to pretend he was uninterested, but he eventually followed at a fast clip.

"I'm running a zoo."

As I walked up the steps, my cell phone rang. No name appeared on caller ID, so I simply said hello.

"Melanie. Sheriff Gallagher here. Heard you've been visiting Ginny."

Drat that Granger. "Just stopped by after church to see if she needed a ride home."

"It would be better if you hung out with your regular friends for a couple of days."

Normally, when the sheriff tells me to butt out, I'm annoyed. His tone was different this time. "Okay. I did say she could call if she needed groceries or something."

"I've been in her house. Looked well-stocked."

He probably wouldn't answer, but I asked anyway. "Can you tell me anything about Janet and what she said about my parents?"

Gallagher was silent for several seconds. "I led her to that topic a couple of times, and she pretty much ignored me. It's...well...it's hearsay, in terms of evidence. I will keep probing and listening."

"I understand we can't get a first-hand account, and I'm willing to accept she had nothing to do with Tom's decisions that night. I just want to know."

"Can see why you would. Now, I have to..."

I interrupted him. "I've assumed all along that she burned those files. Did she?"

"Ongoing investigation. And, say, you were going to bring me a dog bone."

"Cat pushed it off the counter, and Mister Tibbs ate it."

He chuckled. "Don't open a detective agency." He hung up.

I walked to the window and watched both pets sniffing near the mouse hole at the corner of the barn. Gallagher had as much as told me Janet Dodson burned my file boxes. What did I care?

Mister Tibbs' image came to me, and I watched her paw at the soil near the barn. "If they can't get Janet Dodson on an arson charge, maybe they can get her on endangering an animal."

Thinking of Tom Dodson's seeming role in my parents' deaths reminded me of Hal's book. I found it on my dresser and flipped through it. The pseudonyms he used were painfully close to names of real people. Peter Frost had been Mr. Springer, and Hal seemed to be setting Springer up as the murderer.

And maybe it was a set-up. Hal hadn't finished the book. Would he have created a character who owned a grain elevator and dubbed him killer of the fictional Mattie and Adam Durkins? Whatever Hal knew, or thought he knew, he had taken it to his own grave.

CHAPTER TWENTY-FOUR

I SAT IN MY RECLINER early Sunday afternoon and used my phone to study furniture ads. With an impulsive streak unusual for me, I ordered a second recliner, a coffee table, and a credenza-high oak veneer entertainment center.

Then I decided to hook up my small TV and the converter box that let me get over-the-air channels. I had just plugged it in when Sandi called.

Her tone was tentative. "I thought I should wait until after noon, in case, you know, Syl stayed over."

I watched a sunbeam dance across the hardwood floor and laughed. "We almost couldn't wait to get away from each other."

"Oh, that's too bad. I…"

I laughed again. It felt good. "We ate at Mama Sparks' place last night. She must have added something new to the barbeque sauce."

"Gosh, Ryan said the same thing. Are you okay?" Sandi asked.

"Fine. Just not how you want to spend an evening getting to know each other."

"So, other than the bathroom runs, did you two have a good time?"

"Sure. I mean, I've known Syl for what, six or seven months. We were comfortable with each other."

"Comfortable? Is that all?"

I shrugged to myself. "It's good for now. I don't want to rush into anything with someone I could be seeing around town for the rest of my life."

"What?" Sandi paused. "Oh, you mean in case it doesn't work out?"

"Listen to us. Syl and I have had one date. You could run into him again before I do."

"So, he didn't call yet?"

"No reason he should."

"Melanie, you're infuriating."

"If you want me to go all high school on you, it's not going to happen."

She sighed. "Okay. Any big news on the Ginny or Janet front? You wouldn't believe the tight lid the sheriff's office has on all of this."

"Not so much. I stopped by to see Ginny after church, and…"

"You went to church?"

"It's not like the roof falls in. I wanted to check on the idea of the box of cans going missing. It did."

She put on her reporter questioning an interviewee tone. "How did you find out?"

"A new box for cans was in the downstairs hall. Sunday School class made it. When I ran into Mrs. Reilly, she said the other one disappeared."

"She thought it was stolen?"

I could almost see Sandi reach into her purse for a notebook and grinned to myself. "She said she had meant to ask the sheriff if he took it after Tom died. I didn't tell her our bet was that the killer whacked someone with one of the cans and took the box."

"Okay, I'll follow up on that. What did Ginny tell you?"

"Not much. My excuse to visit was to offer her a ride home from the hospital, and…"

"So she's out? Maybe I'll go by her house."

"I was in her room when Granger came to drive her home, supposedly to have her check the house. He stink-eyed me, and later Gallagher called me to tell me to hang out with my usual friends for a while."

Sandi kind of huffed. "They can't tell us who we can talk to."

"True, but I think it's more than them not wanting you to get a story or me to prod her with questions about Tom or Janet Dodson."

"Like what?" Sandi asked.

"My gut says they think she may have had something to do with Tom's death."

"Is that the gut that reacted to Mama Sparks' barbeque or your reporter instincts?"

"I'd like to think my more logical instincts. Ginny talked to me as if she assumed I knew Tom and she had…dated, for lack of a better term."

Sandi did a mini-shriek. "People around town are guessing about that."

I remembered Eliza's comment in the grocery store. "In Hy-Vee one day, Eliza told me she heard Janet insisting Tom get rid of a female staffer. Or something like that."

"What made you think she meant Ginny?"

"She was probably the only woman who worked there, besides when Janet took notes at Tom's meetings."

Sandi and I were silent for several seconds. Then she asked, "Why would Ginny talk to you about that? Because you found her?"

"Not too big a leap of logic. She has to figure people at least suspect an affair. Why else would Janet go after her?" I thought about Ginny's frowning parents. Not likely she would confide in them.

"Well, I have to go by there. If I don't, Ryan will hear she's home, and he'll get the interview."

"Good luck getting through to her."

"I'll call you after I talk to her."

Sandi was optimistic about Ginny opening up to her. If I were Ginny, I'd sleep all afternoon.

WHEN I DIDN'T HEAR from Syl, I began to wonder if Mama Sparks' barbeque still had him occupied. I called him about three o'clock. "How are things at the Seaton Estate?"

"Better. We definitely eat in Fairfield next time."

Next time. "I hear Ryan didn't enjoy the food lately either."

"You don't mind if he's sick, do you?"

"Ha, ha. Anyway, just touching base. Should be at your place one day this week."

"I go up to Des Moines tomorrow morning, but I'm coming back in the evening. Was going to suggest we get together tonight, but probably better wait 'til I get home."

I was mildly disappointed, but didn't want to spend time together if he didn't feel good. "Makes sense. Safe driving."

"Stay out of trouble."

SANDI DIDN'T CALL, PROBABLY BECAUSE she wasn't able to see Ginny. I put a pot of split pea soup on the stove and took Mister Tibbs and Cat for a short walk among the withered corn stalks. I wanted Mister Tibbs to learn how to find the house if she followed Cat into the maze. Cat I didn't worry about.

I made cornbread to go with the soup. When I finished, I spent a solid hour trying to tape together the jillions of pieces of cancelled checks from the Keosauqua account Tom Dodson probably did not share with Janet.

After lots of tape and more than a little cussing, I had a few checks with amount and name of the recipient. Ginny's name was not among them, but the six I could discern were to a jeweler in Iowa City (two), a bed and breakfast in an Amish village, a rental car agency, a boutique in the big mall in Coralville, and (my crowning prize), a car dealer in Des Moines.

No one ever bought me a $28,000 car. More than the money Tom had spent on someone, likely Ginny, was the time away from home. Where did Janet think Tom went the night he stayed at a B&B or the day he went to a car dealer in Des Moines?

"Why rent a car?" Mister Tibbs moved her head off my shoe for a moment but offered no opinion. I supposed Dodson didn't want Janet to notice mileage usage on a family car.

At six-thirty, someone rapped on my side door. Sandi usually went to the front door, but that porch light was off. I'd been so engrossed in taping the checks that I hadn't realized how dark it had grown.

A woman's silhouette made me think Sandi, but I opened the door to Ginny Forman.

"Hi, Melanie."

I stood aside to let her in. How would I keep her from seeing the checks on the dining room table? "Gosh, you must feel a lot better. I'm glad to see that."

"Thanks." She glanced around the kitchen, as I gestured to the table in the corner. "Wow. Look at that pie safe."

"I'll make us some hot tea." I nodded toward the safe as I turned on the faucet. "Belonged to my grandmother. I'm glad my mom kept it."

Mister Tibbs smelled Ginny's shoe and then wandered toward Cat's chair by the window.

Ginny sat. "You're lucky. My mother wants everything modern. Almost antiseptic."

I put the kettle on the stove and sat across from Ginny. "You're okay to drive?"

"I wouldn't get on an interstate, but around here it seems fine."

I took in her blue fleece jacket over a deep purple knit top. "Can I take your coat?"

She shook her head. "Kind of chilly."

I nodded. "Did you find anything taken from your house?"

She had been studying the pie safe and, for a moment, looked puzzled. "Oh, no. Deputy Granger walked me from room to room. I was kind of...irritated, because I knew they had moved stuff around on the desk in the spare room. Later, I could tell someone had been through my drawers."

Probably looking for a murder weapon. "That's weird. I could see them going through Janet's house that way."

She nodded. "I know, right? When I mentioned it, Aaron said they wanted to be sure she hadn't left anything dangerous."

"Like what?"

Ginny shook her head. "I asked him the same thing, but he said I'd have to ask Sheriff Gallagher. I don't care enough to talk to anybody else."

What does she want? I got that Ginny wanted company, but why me? Yes, my pets and I had saved her. Beyond that, we had never hung around together, despite being close in age and both college-educated.

I stood to finish making the tea and was glad I had bought Fig Newtons the other day. "I was about to offer you cookies, but did you eat? I made split pea soup and cornbread."

Her eyebrows went up, and her smile seemed genuine. "I'd love cornbread."

I put a mug of tea in front of her and took the pan of cornbread from my fridge. My concentration on heating the cornbread was so complete that her commanding tone shocked me.

"Melanie, why do you have all of these checks? Tom's checks."

I turned from the counter and met her gaze. Ginny stood in the doorway between the kitchen and dining room, and her deep frown said she was irritated. Or was it scared?

I needed time to think. "Let me put the cornbread on the kitchen table, and we'll talk."

She didn't seem happy with my response, but she returned to the kitchen table and sat.

When I placed the warm cornbread on a plate in front of her, she almost spat her words. "Where did you get those checks? What are you going to do with them?"

"When I saw you in the hospital, I mentioned what Janet said about Tom maybe running my parents off the road almost three years ago."

Ginny came to Tom's defense. "She was definitely lying!" Angry though she was, she took a bite of the cornbread.

I kept my tone measured. "She could have been. And if he did, I doubt it was deliberate. She said he just wanted to talk to my father."

"Tom said your father wanted him to turn the elevator into a co-op. He said your father and some others were pressuring him to sell." Her scowl deepened. "They wanted the profits from the business he built!"

I shook my head. "Tom would have gotten a lot from the sale, and no individual makes money from a co-op. I think Dad and a few others wanted a way to pay less to process their grain." *Because he knew the business would be able to charge less if someone wasn't taking money off the top.*

She folded her arms. "It wasn't their concern. And that still doesn't explain the checks. Did you break into the elevator office?"

"No. I took some bags of trash Janet tossed."

Ginny's mouth formed a silent O.

I continued. "Trash at the curb is on the town's property. It's not stealing." I didn't mention that some of the trash came from the dumpster at the elevator.

Ginny stood and strode to the dining room table. I followed, wishing I had karate training in case her temper turned physical. I stayed several feet behind her.

She stood over the checks, then sat in the chair I had used as I put together the pieces. Her shoulders relaxed. "These are to businesses, not people."

"I know." *I should probably shut up.* Instead, I added, "My guess is he was buying presents for someone."

She reddened. "You don't know that!"

I nodded. "True, but you as much as told me that you two had an affair. And what junior librarian drives a car that costs close to $30,000?"

She pounded her fist on the table with such force that a couple of checks floated to the floor. "I save money!"

"Did you break up with him, or the other way around?"

Fury gone, her eyes filled. "That bitch! She said if he didn't stop seeing the 'little chippy' – that's what she called me – that she'd get more than half of their assets in a divorce."

So, Ginny knew Tom didn't go back to Janet to spend their golden years together, as Janet had said. "So why kill him? Why not her?"

Ginny flushed. "I didn't kill him! He, he fell."

"Uh-huh. I think he fell when a can made contact with his head."

She stood and moved several steps toward me, but stopped and screamed, "You bitch!"

That seemed to be a popular word these days. "Why did you come here, Ginny?"

"Everyone says you're so nosy, even without being a reporter. I wanted to know what you know."

"I don't *know* anything. I'm guessing."

"But you'll tell the sheriff your guesses."

I hoped she didn't decide to keep me from talking to him. "Sheriff Gallagher is a big boy. He'll follow the evidence."

Her eyes strayed to the checks on table. She quickly moved to them and began shuffling the taped checks and many other pieces into a pile on the table. "He won't have this evidence."

I avoided telling her that the bank could provide digital copies of any checks.

"Get me a bag or something!"

I almost smiled. I couldn't figure out why she thought I'd take orders from her in my own home, but I opened the cabinet under the kitchen sink and took out a plastic grocery sack.

When I turned back toward the dining room, I saw why she wanted my attention away from her. The tiny gun in her right hand was a .22 caliber. Small, but any bullet can kill if it goes to the right spot in a body.

"Are you nuts, Ginny?"

"Don't ask me that!"

I shrugged. "Okay. But you don't want to get in more trouble. Put the gun back in your coat pocket."

Her hand shook and tears ran down her cheeks. "He said he wanted his stupid key to the office, that I should come to the church during the talks and meet him in the hall."

I supposed that made some sense. Janet would be in the community room, and Tom wouldn't have to sneak around town to get the key back.

"So why not just give him the key and leave?"

She used the back of the hand with the gun to wipe tears off one cheek. "I was so stupid. So stupid. I told him we should go away together. Just leave. That night."

If she hadn't been pointing the gun at me, I might have felt sorry for Ginny Forman. "What did he say?"

"He said he recommended me for the job at the library and gave me a car. What else did I want?"

"Ouch."

"After everything! We couldn't hang out in town, none of my friends or my parents ever met him. And he thought I would be satisfied with a freaking car?"

Quiet Ginny Forman had a heck of a temper. "He's not worth going to jail over."

Still in the doorway between the kitchen and dining room, she gestured with her gun. "I didn't come here to hurt you, but you've seen those checks. You should go into your basement."

I didn't expect my pets to save me again, and I wasn't about to go someplace that would be convenient for her to shoot me. "I don't think so."

"Do what I said!"

I kept my face impassive. "Or what?"

In response, she raised her left hand to her right and focused the gun on me. I ducked, and her shot went above me and to the left.

Mister Tibbs began barking, and Cat jumped off his chair and ran toward my bedroom.

"Stop shooting, Ginny!"

She aimed for my spot on the floor, and I rolled toward the kitchen table. After she fired again, I ducked and almost dove toward the refrigerator and opened its door. Small protection, but better than none. I picked up a plastic jar of mustard from the fridge door and threw it at her, before I ducked behind the door.

"Ow! I'll get you!" she yelled.

My side door opened and heavy footsteps pounded toward the dining room, where Ginny still stood in the doorway, aiming her gun at me.

"Drop it, Ginny!"

I thought that voice was Newt Harmon's.

"Right now!"

Definitely Aaron Granger.

I stayed behind the refrigerator door, but raised my head to peer toward the dining room. Both men had run toward Ginny, guns drawn. They had on bulletproof vests, but I still thought it was pretty brave.

Ginny shrieked and something metal hit the floor. Her gun, I hoped. Granger and Newt blocked my view.

Mister Tibbs continued barking.

"Quiet, Mister Tibbs! Come here."

She stopped barking. As Granger told Ginny to get on the floor, Mister Tibbs padded into the kitchen and walked into my arms.

Cat sauntered in behind her, as if he had nowhere else to go so he might as well check out things in the kitchen.

CHAPTER TWENTY-FIVE

EVEN I HAD LOST COUNT of how often I'd been in Sheriff Gallagher's office in the last few months. At least this time it wasn't in the middle of the night. Though the chair in front of his desk was no more comfortable than other times.

Ambrose was matter–of-fact about my call. He seemed more concerned about whether a bullet had embedded itself in the dining room wall.

"Don't you want to know if one embedded itself in me?"

"Mel, you wouldn't be the one calling me if it did. Is Syl with you?"

"I didn't call him. I heard Sandi's voice in the lobby, but I doubt Gallagher will let her into his office."

"You need me down there?"

"No. I have Mister Tibbs and Cat locked in my bedroom for now. I may let them both sleep on the bed tonight."

"You wouldn't want any goats, would you?"

"Ambrose! I don't need more animals to feed."

"All you'd do is build a pen. I mean I would, and…"

"No goats!"

Gallagher had been down the hall with Ginny, and now his voice came from behind me. "Melanie. Call Ambrose later."

"Gotta go, Ambrose." I looked at Gallagher as he sat behind his desk. "How'd you know it was him?"

"My wife heard somebody say Sharon told him the goats have to go." He studied me as he sat behind his desk. "I told you to stay out of this."

"She came to my door. How did I know she had a gun?"

He almost smiled. "She might not have used it, if you hadn't had those checks."

I sighed. "There is that. I wasn't expecting her."

"Where'd you get those?"

I shifted in my chair. "Janet's trash."

He swore. "We took her garbage the night of the funeral. You're telling me you'd already been there?"

"Um. I didn't take much. And her cans were on public property."

Gallagher glared at me.

"And isn't there something about not incriminating yourself?" I had decided not to mention the checks were from the Dodson Elevator garbage. I wondered if I could get in trouble for taking trash from the business dumpster.

His broad face reddened. "Dammit, Melanie. Any evidence you took is useless for prosecution!"

"Oh, right. I was, uh, looking for clothes that smelled like smoke. Did you find any?"

He pointed an index finger at me. "None of your damned business!"

It didn't seem like the time to mention I had found the empty Gabapentin bottle. I decided to change the subject. "How come you were following Ginny?"

He frowned. "Because it's *my* job to catch criminals." He paused. "We also figured out that she had visited her parents only on Sunday the weekend Tom was murdered. In her garage, we found the box that used to contain the church's donated canned goods. She had it folded up with her stuff to recycle."

I felt pleased that Sandi and I had thought about the missing box. "I'm glad you had people following her."

He pointed a pencil at me. "You were lucky twice. Next time you may not be."

"I don't plan on a next time."

Behind me, Syl said, "Are you taking bets, Sheriff?"

Gallagher snorted.

I regarded Gallagher and asked, "Did you call Syl?"

"Sandi did." Syl nodded at the sheriff. "I told Sophie you invited me down here."

Gallagher shook his head as he stood. "She usually spots lies better." He gestured toward his door. "Out of here."

Syl laughed. "I'll have to get better at it."

Gallagher said, "I don't want to see either of you down here again anytime soon."

Syl and I said goodbye to Sophie and walked into the crisp evening, toward the parking lot.

"You have your truck?" he asked.

"Yes, it…"

Sandi's voice carried across the parking lot. "Melanie!"

I faced Syl. "If I take five minutes to talk to her, then we'll be on our own."

Quietly, he said, "I'm all for that."

Sandi reached us. "Ginny shot at you in your own house?"

I grinned. "Only a couple of times."

Sandi's expression said she didn't find this funny.

"It'll only take a minute to fill you in."

She scribbled notes, as I gave her the rundown on the night's events. When I finished, I asked, "Where's Ryan?"

Sandi glanced around, then back at Syl and me. "I think he went to Des Moines. He has a job interview tomorrow. "

"Hope he gets it," I said.

"So he'll stop annoying you?" Syl asked.

"Yep."

Sandi studied me. "It means whoever the new editor is will get only me. Well, me and Betty, plus Salty."

"Who are Betty and Salty?" Syl asked.

I answered. "Betty is sort of local social stuff, and Salty photographs high school sports. Pictures sell papers. Anyway, both are very much part-time."

"One more question," Sandi said. "What the hell were you thinking, stealing garbage from Janet's place?"

I shrugged. "I figured right after Tom died she might be throwing out a lot of stuff."

Syl took my hand as we walked toward our trucks, Sandi keeping pace.

"From the sound of things," Syl said, "Janet broke into your house to burn files and later tried to kill Ginny. If she has a good lawyer, he can say she was distraught, and she might not get much of a sentence."

I grimaced. "There's a cheery thought. I could be running into her in Hy-Vee in a few years."

"Or less," Sandi said. "You think they'll have much trouble proving that Ginny killed Dodson?"

I pushed the key fob to open my truck. "They must have suspected her, to be following her this evening."

A sharp bang announced a backfire from Stooper's ancient car. He parked on the street, got out, and pointed a finger at the three of us. "And you didn't call me?"

Sandi spoke quickly. "I did, but I only let it ring a couple times because I got another call."

"And I just walked out of Gallagher's office," I added.

Syl grinned. "My bad."

Stooper stood next to us. "We goin' to Mel's? You gotta catch me up, and we gotta pick a name for the business. Mel's been puttin' it off. If we're all together, we can gang up on her."

Sandi glanced at her watch, and I smiled. "My house has possibly still got deputies roaming around. Let's go to the diner."

TWENTY MINUTES LATER, WE HAD each ordered. Until then, I hadn't realized my stomach had been growling for some time. I had been too absorbed in taping checks and ducking bullets to think about food.

With four of us in one booth – and one of them being Stooper – space was tight. He pulled a wrinkled piece of paper from his pocket. On it were four options for business names.

Mow and Bloom
River's Edge Lawns and More
Clear and Plant
Plants and Pots

I studied the list. "Not bad. I think you've mentioned a couple of those names before."

Stooper nodded. "You never said no to any of my ideas."

Sandi's lips twitched. "We're near the water. What about Surf and Turf?"

Stooper seemed to consider this, then realized she was kidding. "I'm sittin' on the end here. Nobody's leaving until we have a name."

I recognized how important this was to Stooper. And he did more of the physical work than I did. I hadn't expected it to go that way, but we had a lot of jobs now. "Okay. We'll pick a name."

"Tonight?" Syl asked.

The three of us nodded.

"In that case," Syl said, "do you mind a couple other ideas?"

"'Course not," Stooper said.

Syl tilted his head back for a moment, then met my gaze. "Mel's lived here a long time, and she has a reputation in town."

Under her breath, Sandi said, "Uh-oh."

Syl took a pen from his pocket and added to Stooper's list. "What about Law'N Order? Or maybe Lawn Enforcement?"

"Or Mulch Maiden," Sandi added.

Stooper had picked up on the humor. "Can't be Maiden. I'd be out."

"It isn't going to be," I began.

"Or the Lawn Ranger," Syl said.

Sandi laughed so hard she put her head on her folded arms.

Syl grinned. "We'd have more ideas if Shirley were here."

Stooper had gone quiet. I didn't want him to think we were making fun of him. "Okay, you guys are as funny as rubber crutches. Stooper, I like your ideas."

"Which one do you like best?"

Syl and Sandi seemed to recognize that Stooper could think we were mocking him.

"Well, Clear and Plant is a lot of what we do," I said.

"Especially at my place," Syl said.

I frowned. "I like plants and pots, but we'd catch a ration with people taking the 's' off pots."

"You could put a marijuana leaf on your truck," Syl said.

In a serious tone, Stooper said, 'I'm not sure we'd get the kind of clients we want."

I hid a smile. "True. I guess I'd go with River's Edge Lawns and More."

Syl frowned. "What if you get jobs in other towns?"

I shrugged. "River's Edge is where we live, and it tells people how to find us."

Syl grinned. "RELAM. Mel's on the lam. Gallagher's after her."

Sandi wiped her eyes on a napkin."

Stooper grinned. "I kind of like that."

"If we've named the business, what about that rascal cat?" Syl asked.

"He was hell-bent on saving Mel," Stooper said. "What about Hell Bent?"

Sandi rolled her eyes. "You couldn't exactly go around yelling that name."

"Okay. H.B. for short," Stooper said.

"Stooper, you named the business." I nodded to Syl. "You just named Cat. He's now Rascal."

AFTER OUR LATE DINNER, Stooper might have come back to the farm, but Sandi took his elbow and directed him toward their cars.

My truck was next to Syl's, in front of the diner. He glanced at Sandi and Stooper's backs. "You think you'll need help putting stuff in order at your place?"

I smiled. "Why don't you just come on over?"

He grinned. "I do believe I'll do that."

CHAPTER TWENTY-SIX

AS THE ELEMENTARY SCHOOL BUS rumbled past the hardware store Monday morning, a couple kids pressed their Halloween masks to the window and waved to me. A fun school day for them, hectic for the teachers.

I whistled as I put a decorative bale of hay and a couple more pumpkins in the back of my truck. Festive, that was my mood.

I smiled to myself. Syl and I had spent a fun night together. Really fun. For the fifth time, I reminded myself that despite having met him months ago, I barely knew him. But what I knew, I liked. Really liked.

He had left early to drive to Des Moines, but he planned to come back in the late afternoon. We were going to pass out Halloween candy from his house. Unknown to him, I planned to set up a decorative display of pumpkins and dried corn near his front porch.

I had asked Stooper to help me. I thought Syl and I were the first new friends he had made in years, and I wanted to tell him I'd been seeing Syl. No, that was a stupid way to put it. I'd have to think about wording. *Supposedly, you're a word person, Melanie.*

My cell phone rang as I started my truck. Caller ID indicated *The South County News*, so I said, "Hi Sandi."

The deep male chuckle announced Doc Shelton. "Melanie, I see you've maintained your ties to the paper."

"Sandi and I were going to schedule lunch one day this week. How are you, Sir?"

"How about lunch with me? At Mama Sparks' place?"

"Uh, lunch tomorrow would be good, but maybe not there. My stomach didn't like the food Saturday night."

"It's up and down at that place. Today doesn't work for you?"

I hated to tell Doc Shelton no, but I wasn't dressed to eat out, even in River's Edge, and I wanted to focus on Halloween. "If it's urgent, no problem."

"Oh, not really urgent. I wanted to run something by you."

I thought I knew what was coming, and I wasn't interested. To emphasize the inconvenience of meeting him, I said, "If it can't be over the phone, I can go home and change."

The squeak that came through the phone told me Doc Shelton had leaned back in the ancient leather chair in the paper's small conference room. "Okay, here's the deal."

I almost laughed at hearing the elderly doctor use modern slang.

"The thing is, Melanie, the advisory committee members haven't been satisfied with applicants for the editor's job. There's even been talk, I hate to say it, of closing the paper. Maybe ask the Keosauqua paper to have a River's Edge column and..."

"Close the paper? Just because the first round of applicants wasn't what you wanted?"

He sighed. "It's also we weren't what they wanted. Moving expenses, a higher salary than we anticipated."

Was he saying I wasn't worth much?

"You see," Doc Shelton continued, "you're here, you own property. You wouldn't need thousands in moving expenses or a salary to support buying a place. Frankly, the paper just doesn't bring in the ad revenue it used to."

I said nothing for several seconds. "Did you ask Sandi?"

"She made it clear several times that she's not interested. And frankly, I think we might lose Ryan. We need another experienced head here."

I watched bright red maple leaves mix with a bunch of brown oak leaves and shuffle across the street in front of the hardware store. "I'm not sure that's such a great loss."

"He told me you weren't happy with some of his work."

I admired Doc Shelton for providing leadership at the paper since Hal died. When he had signed onto Hal's advisory group more than a year ago, he thought he'd come to a couple of meetings a year. Instead, for months, he had met at least weekly with Scott Holmes and the staff. And Doc didn't have a lot of free time.

"I don't want to be coy with you, Doc. I like my landscaping work. And Ambrose and I have the farm back." My words trailed off.

"Just think about it. You could bring in more advertising revenue, and you and Sandi work well together."

"She said you were thinking of going down to two issues per week."

He sighed. "That would be up to the editor. If she or he can cover the cost of three issues, more power to her."

I didn't want Sandi to lose her job, she'd move. "I need to think about this. And maybe talk to Stooper, and, um, a couple other people."

His smile came through the phone. "Salty said he saw you and that nice Mr. Seaton at the movies in Fairfield Saturday night."

"Oh, good."

"And he told Shirley."

Doc said we should talk salary. I told him I had a lot to think about, promised to call him tomorrow, and hung up. Better not go to the diner to do any thinking.

As I drove toward Syl's, my festive mood hadn't exactly fizzled, but it had lost some of its sparkle.

I had liked working at the paper, except when Hal was on a yelling spree. But be tied to a desk again? Of course, news reporting wasn't as confining as some office work. But the editor role would keep me indoors a lot.

Mentally I went through a typical work week. Maybe two issues would be manageable for me. A lot of my decision would depend on Stooper. Would he want to take over much of the daily work of River's Edge Lawns and More? He already did a lot of it, plus he had a lot less grave marker work.

What about Mister Tibbs and Cat? I had no pets when I worked at the paper previously. Oh, I'd be the editor. I could allow pets in the office. Maybe Cat would want to hang out at Mr. Patel's place during the day. I laughed.

Instead of going straight to Syl's, I stopped by the farm to pick up my pets. Mister Tibbs watered the bale of hay I placed by Syl's porch, so I doused them with water from the outside spigot.

As I placed pumpkins on newspapers, my phone rang again.

Sandi was nearly breathless. "Tell me you said yes."

"I said I'd think about it. Would they really shut down the paper if I said no?"

Her silence told me Sandi had not heard this option. "Uh, maybe Doc just said that so I'd say yes."

She lowered her voice. "Ryan thinks he got that job."

"Music to my ears."

"You could fire him if he doesn't get it."

"Oh, that'd be a great way to start." I sighed. "I said I'd think about it."

"Think the right way." She hung up.

My animals and I sat on the porch, newspapers catching goo from the pumpkins as I carved. Cat tried to act indifferent, but he enjoyed using a claw to pull pumpkin seeds from the pulp.

Stooper pulled into Syl's driveway and stopped short of the house. His car has taken to running its engine for about fifteen seconds after he turns off the ignition. Then it belches.

Mister Tibbs was at his side as soon as he got out of the car. Stooper grinned at me. "You think she'd like me as much if I didn't carry these little bones?" He tossed one toward the porch and Mister Tibbs took off after it.

I stood and brushed my damp hands on my jeans. "You also throw balls."

Stooper climbed the steps and regarded the pumpkins. "Are you going for crooked smiles?"

I sat in one of the wooden porch chairs. "Would you believe me if I said yes?"

"Probably not." He sat next to me and stared at the front yard as he spoke. "Heard you might take over at the paper."

"Jeez. I told Doc Shelton I'd think about it. I actually wanted to talk to you about it."

"Why me?"

I gestured broadly to the now manicured lawn we had created from overgrown bushes and weeds. "We've been growing the business. How do you feel about doing more of the work? A lot more."

"Huh. I figured you was going to say we were done."

That surprised me. "I like this work. I guess...well, Doc Shelton more or less said they might shut it down if they can't find an editor kind of soon."

"Without you," Stooper added. "They asked you to be, what do you call it, interim editor when Hal died."

"And I said no. I like to write articles more than I'd like to manage a paper." I picked up a pumpkin seed and tossed it to Rascal-the-Cat at the other end of the porch. "But I don't want the *South County News* to go away. If it hadn't been here, I wouldn't have moved back home. I'd have stayed in Iowa City or someplace bigger."

Stooper watched Rascal swat the seed. "I like the work, but I don't want to do the paperwork. Or go look for clients."

I smiled at him. "I hear you. So if I do billing and stuff, you'd do most of the backbreaking stuff?"

"Yeah. I need to save for a new car. Could use the work."

"Hmm. Maybe I should get a car, and you could have my truck."

"Huh. Would hafta haul more tools. You usually bring 'em."

I glanced sideways and observed Stooper grinning, not at anything in particular. "What's so funny?"

"Sandi said, if I talked you into taking over at the paper, she'd buy me breakfast at the diner for a week."

I shook my head. "She's a piece of work. But I think I still need to talk to..." I stopped. I hadn't told Stooper Syl and I were dating.

"Ambrose?" Stooper asked.

"I'll mostly tell Ambrose, not ask what he thinks."

"Syl, then."

I nodded. "Listen, I wanted to tell you something. Syl and I are kind of dating."

Stooper laughed. "You think that's news? He's been trying to figure how to ask you out for months."

"What? How come I didn't know that?"

Stooper pulled Mister Tibbs onto his lap. "If you're going to take over at the paper, you oughta get a better nose for news."

I suppose I should.

AUTHOR BIO

Demise of a Devious Suspect is the third book of Elaine L. Orr's River's Edge cozy mystery series, set along the Des Moines River in Southeast Iowa. She also writes the eleven-book Jolie Gentil series, set at the Jersey shore, and the Logland series, set in rural Illinois. For more on her work, visit www.elaineorr.com.

Melanie's Food Favorites

Spaghetti and Chicken Casserole

Ingredients

1 12 ounce package of spaghetti
6 cups cubed cooked chicken breast
2 (10¾ ounce) condensed cream of chicken soup, undiluted
1 (16 oz) sour cream
1 cup chicken broth
1 teaspoon seasoning salt
¼ teaspoon pepper
⅛ teaspoon cayenne pepper
2 Tablespoons dried parsley
Topping:
2 cups sharp cheddar cheese
½ cup bread crumbs or dry stuffing mix
½ cup grated Parmesan cheese (optional)

Instructions

Preheat oven to 350 degrees. Break the spaghetti and cook according to package directions until al dente. Drain. In a large bowl combine cream of chicken soup, sour cream, chicken broth, seasoning salt, pepper, cayenne pepper, and dried parsley. Add cooked spaghetti and chicken. Toss until coated.

Place the mixture in a 9x13 pan that is lightly coated with cooking spray. Top with sharp cheddar cheese. Combine parmesan cheese and bread crumbs and sprinkle on top.

Cover with foil and bake for 40-45 minutes. Take foil off the last ten minutes to make it bubbly.

Banana Bread

Ingredients

1 cup sugar
½ cup (one stick) butter, softened
2 large eggs
1 ½ cups mashed, ripe bananas (3-4 medium)
½ cup milk
1 tsp vanilla
2 ½ cups flour
1 tsp salt (optional)
1 cup chopped walnuts (optional)

Instructions

Lower oven rack so top of pan will be in center of the oven. Preheat oven to 350 degrees. Grease bottom of loaf pan(s). Use one standard bread loaf pan (9 inch), two smaller loaf pans (8 inch), or three mini-loaf pans.

Mix sugar and softened butter, add eggs, and mix. Add mashed bananas, milk, and vanilla. Beat until smooth.

Add flour and salt and mix.

Stir in nuts.

Bake in 9-inch pan about 1¼ hours, 8-inch pan about 1 hour, mini pans about ¾ hour. Center should be clean if tested with a toothpick or top should spring to the touch. Cool on wire racks.

Made in the USA
Lexington, KY
26 November 2018